SWEET WATER VET: TAKING RACHAEL

Dawn Forrest

EROTIC ROMANCE

Siren Publishing, Inc.
www.SirenPublishing.com

A SIREN PUBLISHING BOOK
IMPRINT: Erotic Romance

SWEET WATER VET: TAKING RACHAEL
Copyright © 2011 by Dawn Forrest

ISBN-10: 1-61034-018-3
ISBN-13: 978-1-61034-018-2

First Printing: January 2011

Cover design by Jinger Heaston
All cover art and logo copyright © 2011 by Siren Publishing, Inc.

Printed in the U.S.A.

PUBLISHER
Siren Publishing, Inc.
www.SirenPublishing.com

DEDICATION

To Richard, for being my rock and a hard place.

To Des, for coffee and camaraderie in Cape Town.

SWEET WATER VET: TAKING RACHAEL

DAWN FORREST
Copyright © 2011

Chapter 1

Rachael was enjoying the journey immensely. She had been prepared for a cramped, uncomfortable and noisy flight from London to Houston but instead was experiencing the pleasures of business class. She had been unexpectedly upgraded from the overbooked economy section, and it had taken all her self-control not to do a little victory foot stamp at the check-in desk. This time, it had certainly paid off to dress smartly.

Trying not to appear like Elly May Clampett of *The Beverly Hillbillies*, she thoroughly explored the seat position options, accepted the offered champagne, and watched three of the latest movies. She was sorely tempted to try the complimentary face fresheners and moisturizer, but she didn't like using anything other than hypoallergenic unperfumed products and a little natural vanilla oil on her sensitive skin. When she was too tired to keep her eyes open, she reclined the seat into the flat sleeping position and curled up with a pillow and blanket for a snooze. When they arrived in Houston, she felt relatively refreshed although the time difference of six hours was sure to catch up with her.

In Houston, she caught a much smaller plane for the one-hour flight to Ridge Water, in Meadow Ridge County. It was packed with students, and a party atmosphere prevailed due to their success on the football field. She enjoyed chatting to some of the players who kept asking her to repeat words so that they could listen to her crisp English accent. In turn, she loved hearing that sexy Texan drawl, redolent of warm lazy evenings and jasmine-scented twilights on her grandmother's veranda.

When the plane finally landed and she disembarked, she felt the warm air wrap around her like a snug blanket. It was April, and it felt distinctly weird to step out of a cool, air-conditioned plane into warm air instead of the other way around. She detected a faint smell of soil, dust and grass, of home. With a glad heart and a spring in her step, she headed for the terminal building.

Rachael couldn't repress a wide smile when she saw the first of her bags appear on the small carousel. It had a distinctive black-and-white Friesian cow design that she thought was quite fitting for a vet.

"Excuse me, sorry, excuse me, that's my bag," she said in clipped, precise tones as she pushed her way through the crowd to the conveyor belt.

In one smooth move, she confidently grabbed the heavy suitcase and, with only a little difficulty, swung it onto her trolley, grateful that she regularly lifted weights. One bag down, two to go.

While keeping an eye on the carousel, she scanned the room of Meadow Ridge County's small local airport, looking for her cousin, Colin, who had planned to meet her. She was excited to be back in this unusual and contradictory place. The population appeared conservative, yet a surprising number chose to have unconventional relationships. Colin was a good example. He was a professional, ethical person who happened to be in a ménage relationship with his best friend Mark and their wife Susan. They didn't publicize their life choices but got on with the day-to-day business of living in an accepting, nonjudgmental environment. Local amateur historians theorized that, in the old days, when women were few and times were hard, it had made sense to share. It improved the odds of survival. Whatever the original reasons were, the practice hadn't died out.

Rachael had grown up in one of the more conventional households on the outskirts of the town of Ridge Water with her mom, dad, and older twin brothers, Cameron and Liam. When she was twelve years old, her father had inherited a farm in Oxfordshire, England, and the family had decided to relocate. Rachael and her brothers had stayed in England to complete their education, but they all had very fond memories of the Texan town and had often spoken casually about returning.

Rachael had always had an affinity for animals, so when she heard that Colin had decided to study veterinary science it gave her the idea to do the same. After graduating from university, she'd worked in several practices in England, specializing in livestock. She enjoyed her work— absolutely loved it. Apart from her family, it was the most important thing in her life, and that was the problem. She had hoped that, by now, at the age of twenty-eight, she would have found someone special who meant more to her than her career. She wanted marriage, kids, and the whole nine yards but couldn't see it happening if she stayed put. Her social life had become a little stodgy, so she had decided to be proactive and initiate a complete change of scene. Where better than Meadow Ridge County, Texas, and the big, sunny open spaces of her childhood?

Rachael had e-mailed Colin, hinting at her possible return, and he had suggested that she come home and stay with his family, at least until she decided what she wanted to do. He had even offered her a position as an assistant in his veterinary practice until she became licensed by the American Medical Veterinary Association, a relatively straightforward conversion procedure given her existing qualifications and experience. She'd sent off the application forms some weeks ago and hoped that it wouldn't be too long before she was licensed to practice independently.

While she searched for Colin, Rachael found herself continually tracking back to the tall, broad man standing head and shoulders above most of the people in the room. Even from a distance of about twenty yards, she sensed his presence. It was clear that he was having an effect on other people in the vicinity because, although space was at a premium, people seemed to unconsciously give him room. She didn't think that he was classically handsome and definitely was not a pretty boy. To her, he looked strong, hard, very masculine, and darkly attractive. Unfortunately, he was scowling and appeared irritated, which added to the overall effect of a brooding, dominant male. His eyes roamed the area clearly looking for someone and—as if drawn by Rachael's inspection—locked on hers. For a few long seconds, she couldn't look away and felt a tingle down her spine. When she finally broke eye contact and turned her head toward the conveyor belt, she could still feel the scrutiny of that gaze.

* * * *

Joshua hated crowded places, and the little airport was heaving. The small, twin-propeller aircraft that had just landed had been carrying the high school football team returning from Houston, and it seemed as if the world and his brother had come to meet them. At six feet seven inches tall, Joshua Ryden could easily look over the heads of folks milling around, meeting friends, or waiting for their baggage. He was searching for Rachael Harrison, the woman he had agreed to collect but whom he hadn't seen for sixteen years, when he had been a lanky sixteen-year-old boy and she a pudgy twelve-year-old girl. He hadn't really paid attention to her then, and she was bound to have changed.

Damn it. He really wanted to get back to the ranch quickly. He was worried about his prize bull. It had a high temperature that morning and had stumbled in the stall, which had alerted the foreman that something was amiss. Colin, his preferred vet, had agreed to come out to the ranch provided that Joshua filled in for him and collected his cousin from the airport. Joshua had suggested that he could send a ranch hand instead, but Colin was adamant that if Joshua didn't go then he himself would. Colin didn't trust anyone else with his cousin, and Joshua didn't trust anyone else with his bull, so here he was, suffering a crowd of mostly strangers to meet someone he didn't *really* know. *Great*.

When he first saw the woman at the carousel, he dismissed her. She was not what he was expecting. If that was Rachael Harrison, then she had grown up like a signet to a swan, no longer the soft rounded child he vaguely remembered but a strong and confident-looking person. With a mop of short, tight, honey-coloured curls on her head, she was the most naturally attractive woman he had ever seen. He noted her clothes—soft black leggings hugging shapely legs fitted into black leather knee high boots and a long, tight, fitted white cotton T-shirt covered with an expensive-looking rich brown leather jacket. His mother would have called it "layers," describing how people dressed in unpredictable weather. If her different attire hadn't given him a clue, then the clinching factor would have been her pale skin. Her face had an almost porcelain complexion, except for the smattering of freckles across her cheekbones and nose. *Yep, she's from a country where the sun doesn't shine.*

* * * *

Out of the corner of her eye, she saw Mr. Tall-'n-Broad moving in her direction but was distracted when her phone bleeped, indicating an SMS. After liberating it from the crowded depths of her handbag, she saw that the message had been sent some time ago, but as she had switched on her phone only when the plane landed, she was receiving it now. The message read, "Really sorry; emergency with work; ranch owner Joshua Ryden coming to pick you up instead. He's tall, dark brown hair, blue eyes; can't miss him. C U soon. Who's your favorite cousin?" Rachael couldn't help but grin at the old joke between her and Colin, but then, as her brain caught up with the new information, she was suddenly confronted by a wall of checked cotton shirt: Mr. Tall-'n-Broad.

"Ma'am, are you Rachael Harrison?" the shirt said in a low, deep drawl.

Rachael froze for a second, as the rich bass tones of that voice formed images of melted chocolate on warm skin. She slowly looked up past an imposing chest, a closely shaved square set jaw finished with a cleft chin, a wide mouth, and a slightly crooked nose, possibly broken in the past, into the most piercing blue eyes she had ever seen on a human. They reminded her of a Malamute she had once treated. *Oh, woof. Hello, big fellow.*

Captivated, she became aware of his alluring masculine scent, evocative of fresh hay, warm earth, leather and sex. *Mmm, yum.*

"Are you Rachael Harrison?" he repeated carefully.

She stepped back to protect her personal space but instantly regretted it. "Yes. Yes, I am, and you must be," she looked at her phone again, "Joshua Ryden. I'm very pleased to meet you."

She stuck out her hand, but when his skin touched hers, she felt a jolt.

"Oops, static electricity," she muttered, silently wondering how that was possible when they stood on rubber tiles and she was wearing natural fibers.

* * * *

His irritation at being away from the ranch melted with her smile. Close up, she was even more gorgeous, and that crisp, no-nonsense British accent turned him on. Recovering, he remembered his manners.

"Yep, I'm pleased to meet you too, Rachael." She had a good, firm handshake. He liked a woman with a strong grip. "Do all of your bags look like this?" He raised his eyebrow mockingly as he nodded toward her cow-style case.

"Yes," she sighed wearily, as if expecting a ribbing. "And I am aware they look silly, bordering on the ridiculous. My brothers never fail to point it out. I bought the set for several reasons. They are easy to spot, difficult to mistake or steal. They are good quality, and…make me smile." She looked up at him as if challenging him to deny her logic.

"Well, I'll just rope these in then," he said, amused by her quirky explanation. Hiding a grin, he quickly reached passed her to the carousel and grabbed the two remaining bags as they trundled passed. He placed them on the trolley as if they weighed nothing at all. "Follow me."

Without further ado, he took control of the trolley and strode purposely toward the main doors, with people parting like the Red Sea before Moses.

* * * *

As she followed in his wake, she was treated to a better view of the whole package. His shirt hung fairly loose, providing only a tantalizing hint of the hard body underneath. As he walked, Rachael was mesmerised by the way his jeans rode on his ass. *Lord, he's sex on legs.* She didn't bother chiding herself because she suspected most women between the ages of eighteen and eighty would think the same thing, so she couldn't be held responsible for the salacious thoughts running through her head. As if on cue, several women turned their heads to track his progress across the room.

When they got to the outside doors, he glanced back at her. "Wait here," he commanded and then walked outside.

Rachael stood waiting as instructed. Three minutes later, a huge utility vehicle—UV—pulled up and he jumped out.

"I don't know," she said, shaking her head and indicating the bags and then the UV. "I don't think they'll all fit."

He frowned, looking confused.

"It was a joke." She rolled her eyes. "Cars are a lot smaller where I've been living."

He nodded. Did she see a tiny hint of a smile? She wasn't sure.

"I'll take those." He grabbed a case in each hand and placed them in the trunk. She was about to throw the third bag in when his big hand wrapped around hers and the handle. "I said I'll do it."

For a second, she held on but then saw the determined look on his face and relented. This wasn't something to get into a battle of wills over— not with this guy who seemed more than capable of disarming her. A little taken aback because she wasn't used to taking orders, she nevertheless said graciously, "Thank you. I'm just used to doing stuff myself."

He straightened up and handled the case with an ease that she envied. Rachael thought that it must be great to have that kind of strength and not give it a second thought. He opened the passenger door and lent her his arm to climb in. She was immediately aware of the restrained power behind his gentle grip and felt a little fizzle of excitement at the base of her spine. She realised that, despite his stern and rather bossy manner, he was behaving like a gentleman. Then she caught him briefly eyeing her ass and biting his bottom lip. *Well, maybe not totally.* Her interest in him increased.

He quickly looked away as she bounced down on the grey leather bench seat and looked about the vehicle. Everything here was much bigger than she was used to—the cars, the sky, even the man now climbing into the driver's side.

He explained why he was collecting her, "I expect that you're tired, so I'm sorry, but we needed Colin. One of our bulls has a problem." He looked concerned. "It's important that we get him healthy again quickly. We planned to," he paused, "never mind."

"What?" she automatically asked.

He looked awkward for a moment. "We planned to collect semen in four days time for AI."

"Oh, no worries. I'm a vet. I understand."

Rachael had worked for a few months with a mobile bovine artificial insemination unit in England, so the thought of it didn't faze her at all, and she was mildly amused by his reaction. She wished she'd had the guts to feign ignorance and asked him to explain, just for fun.

"Is that so?" he said, now looking impressed and relieved.

"Yes, I'll be helping Colin out."

As they drove away from the airport, she looked out of the window and tried to find something she recognized.

"It all seems vaguely familiar, yet I don't actually recognize anything yet," she murmured, lost in thought. "I was twelve when I left, and I'm just realizing that twelve-year-olds don't pay much attention to scenic details or the spaces between destinations."

She gazed out of the window, noting the prickly pear cacti. They were growing in clumps along fence lines and against old wooden posts bleached gray by the elements. It was April, and the wildflowers on the road verges were blooming. Rachael thought that the road looked like a scarf with multicoloured edges winding over the rolling distant hills. On one of those hills, she could see an oil pumpjack, the type aptly named a nodding donkey.

"It is very different from England," he said, keeping his eyes on the road. "I was there about ten years ago."

"How was it?"

"Wet."

She chuckled. "You obviously didn't catch the two weeks of sunshine. The big blue Texan sky is what I've missed most," she added wistfully. He briefly turned to look at her, his expression warming with a smile. *Wow, I'd have missed big, blue Texan eyes if I'd known about them.* She changed the subject. "Are you taking me to your ranch?"

"Yep. I hope you don't mind. Colin thought it was the best idea because no one is home at the moment. Susan is teaching and Mark is flying."

"No, it'll be interesting to see what I'll be working with."

"What?" He sounded surprised. "You intend to work with livestock here?"

"Yes, why? Did you expect cats and rats only, or dogs and frogs if I'm lucky?" She couldn't help her sarcasm.

"No, not really. It's just that cattle and horses are difficult physical work, and I don't know of any other lady livestock vets in the area."

She regarded him coolly. "There's always a first."

"Well, good luck with that, but you may find that some of the ranchers, particularly the old boys, will be hard on you just for being a woman."

"And what about you, Mr. Ryden? Will you be hard on me?" She was irritated but still couldn't help being provocative. She didn't think that the innuendo would be lost on him.

"Well, that depends," he drawled.

"On what?"

"On how good you are."

"Good enough."

She left it up to him to determine what she meant. The conversation ended, but Rachael noted that his knuckles were white as he gripped the steering wheel tightly. She was now starting to feel a little tired but couldn't nap, not with this man sitting so close. First, he unsettled her too much, and, second, who wanted to be caught drooling by an attractive man? And she did find him attractive. Compellingly so. It was just plain odd because she didn't know him at all. *He's so...manly* was the only lame explanation she could come up with. If things followed their normal pattern of events, then he would soon bore the socks off her. He wouldn't get as far as the pants. *Pity, really.*

The UV passed under a metal arch made up of the words *Sweet Water Ranch,* and deep vibrations reverberated in the cab as they went over a cattle grid. Fifteen minutes later, they drove into the ranch yard. There were farm buildings, paddocks, and what looked like a bunkhouse. Set off much farther to one side was a beautiful large two-story house with a wide veranda.

"It is lovely," she sighed.

"It's home."

His voice and face softened. It took her breath away.

Joshua parked the truck in front of the house and quickly got out and around the vehicle to open her door. He helped her out with his big hand lingering on her elbow as she dropped her feet to the ground. She felt the warmth of his open palm and fractionally leaned into it.

"Thanks," she murmured, and for a long moment they stood still, neither wanting to break contact.

"Rach," someone called, breaking the spell. "Rachael!" She turned toward the voice.

"Hey, Colin!" she shouted and sprinted across the yard into his open arms. He swung her around.

"It's so good to see you, Rach. Five years is too long. I was about to come and visit you again."

"Oh no, I don't think my local pub would cope." She laughed. "They still talk about 'that crazy Yank.'"

"Ah, they're just jealous that I could lasso that cow." They both laughed.

"The years have been kind," she said, pinching his cheek. "You're looking good. I'm thinking that marriage agrees with you."

"That it does, that is does," he chuckled. "And you look beautiful. I can't believe you've managed to stay single. What are those English guys thinking?"

"Well, I'm picky. You know how I am about choosing clothes, and they only go *on* my body."

He laughed. "There's plenty to choose from in Meadow Ridge, if you're interested."

She looked toward Joshua, who was standing with another man.

"So I see."

Colin made the introductions when they neared the men.

"Cousin, you've already met Joshua Ryden. This is his brother, James."

Have I died and gone to hunk heaven? Are there no average-looking blokes here? James Ryden was at least six feet three, with a body and face any model would be happy to own. He was fairer than was his brother, with golden brown, sun-streaked, close-cut curly hair. His features were similar, but a little fresher, softer, and more symmetrical. From the smile on his lips and the twinkle in his eye, Rachael guessed that charm came easily. James was about to speak, but Joshua brusquely cut in.

"Stop flirting before you even start. How's the bull?"

"All fine. Colin can explain everything to you. I'll take care of Rachael." He smirked at Joshua and winked at Rachael. "C'mon, we'll get some coffee. You must be tired after your journey."

He raised his eyebrows in surprised when his brother cut in. "We'll all get some coffee."

Joshua placed himself between them as they walked toward the house. Rachael saw the quick glare he shot at James and the fake, confused what-have-I-done expression he received in return.

Business came first, and Colin explained that the bull had picked up a bacterial infection through a small cut on the leg.

"His body's fighting it, but I've given him a broad spectrum antibiotic that should help to do the job faster. It's nothing too serious."

"What about Thursday? Will he be all right for the collection?"

"Should be, but I admit I'm concerned. I'm not sure that the normally used artificial vagina is best way of collecting this time, especially given the sore leg."

"What's the alternative? We've made a commitment, and I don't want to let anyone down." Joshua looked troubled.

"Well, instead of using an AV we could use the electro-ejaculation technique, but it's technical and I've never done it before."

"Do you know anyone who can?"

"I'll have to ring around."

"That's not necessary. I hadn't planned on working so soon, but if you can get the equipment, I can do it," Rachael said.

The men turned to look at her with serious, yet surprised, expressions.

"That bull is worth nearly a million dollars," Joshua said.

It was Rachael's turn to be surprised. *Does it have platinum balls?*

"He's part of a breeding program, and, as you know, it takes generations of selective breeding to produce an animal of his caliber. His offspring are well sought after," Colin explained.

"I can do it. I spent three months doing it, and I assure you that I know a bull's arse from its elbow, or, more specifically, hock cap."

"If you mess up, you'll be finished as a vet in Meadow Ridge County. News travels fast here. Are you sure you want to risk it?" Joshua said, studying her intently, making it clear that not only his animal but also her career was at stake.

"Look, there is always an element of risk in any procedure, but I am more than capable of doing it, and I'll expect more livestock work to come my way if I do."

For a moment, there was an uneasy quiet as the men considered their options.

"Give her a chance," Colin said. "I'll be there too."

Joshua took a deep breath and nodded, "We'll discuss it over coffee."

They entered the house and sat at a large breakfast bar in a huge kitchen with all the modern conveniences. A friendly, middle-aged Mexican lady came in.

"You want me to make coffee, Mr. James?" she asked with a thick Spanish accent.

"No, it's okay, Isabella. I'll get these, thanks. This is Rachael Harrison, the new vet and Colin's cousin. Rachael, this is Isabella Mendez, our housekeeper and general domestic savior." James introduced them.

"It's nice to meet you, Isabella." Rachael nodded and smiled at the older woman.

"*Encantada*," she replied before bustling out again.

James talked to Rachael as he made the coffee. "Y'know, we were in the same year at elementary school, but you were in a different class."

"Really? I don't remember clearly. Did you pull my hair?"

"I plead the Fifth."

"You can plead whatever you want. It won't save you. They do say that vengeance is a dish best served cold," she joked.

He laughed and held up a mug. "Let me guess." He deliberately glanced down at himself and slightly opened his arms. "You like medium-light with a little sugar?"

Rachael realized that James was a tease. *Well, two can play at this little game.* "Not usually, but I don't mind if there's nothing else. I prefer mine strong, dark and definitely not sweet." She let her gaze wander to Joshua and then back to James, smiling innocently at him. "In fact, right now I need a big one."

James's mouth fell open, and for a few seconds, he was lost for words. Then he laughed. "I can give you that, sweetheart." He turned to the pot, grinning.

Joshua shifted his stance and looked a little uncomfortable. For a brief moment, Rachael wondered if she had overstepped the line and that her teasing had annoyed him. Then she noticed the impressive-looking bulge in his pants and understood that wasn't the case. She quickly snapped her gaze up to his face, swallowed down a gulp and feigned a look of polite inquiry.

He cleared his throat. "About the procedure...what's needed?"

She immediately slipped into no-nonsense business mode. "Well, apart from the probe, which Colin will have to arrange to be couriered, you'll need a cattle pen that is capable of being opened at the sides because, if the bull has problems standing afterward, it might need to be released quickly. I also don't want a head bail with choke bars because it could put pressure on the animal's spine."

"Not a problem. We can do that."

Rachael explained the procedure in a matter-of-fact, professional manner, highlighting the pros and cons, reassuring them that it was the best option for a bull with an injured leg.

"I'd better take a look at him to determine what size of probe we'll need."

As Joshua led the way to the barn, Colin walked with Rachael and leaned in close so that only she could hear his words. "Are you sure that you can handle this? I wouldn't want to lose good clients like the Rydens," he whispered apologetically.

"Don't worry. I've done it lots of times." She thumped his back reassuringly.

When she saw the bull, she nearly had second thoughts. He was a huge beast, and she judged that her arm would only just be long enough.

"Well, this is an easy call. We'll need the biggest probe. Can you get one in time, Colin?"

"Yep. Mark can courier us one in from Houston. He's making a delivery there tomorrow, as luck would have it."

"Super. Are you still okay with me doing it, Joshua? I wouldn't want to force my services on you."

* * * *

She looked at him with just a ghost of a smile on her lips. Joshua wondered if she was playing with him. It was a novel experience, as most people tended to err on the side of caution when dealing with him, and a lot of women were just plain unsettled by his size and character. Her words conjured a plethora of images regarding the various ways she could service him and, though he couldn't be sure, he had the impression that she knew what he was thinking. He tried to concentrate on ranch business and not his increasing interest in Rachael and the pounding in his pants.

"I'll give you a chance, Rachael, trusting that you are, in fact, good enough." He echoed her words from the conversation in his UV. She nodded and gave him a genuine smile, which soften his hardened, and, if he were honest, lonely heart.

As they finished their coffee, he noticed that she looked a little drained. No doubt she was feeling the tiring effects of her long journey. That, together with the fact that Colin was clearly desperate to catch up with family news, had him wrapping up their business conversation quickly.

Watching them go, James turned to Joshua. "An intriguing woman."

"You blatantly seemed to think so."

"Well, you can't blame a guy for trying, but I have to say, brother, I've never seen a woman less interested in me and more interested in you. No offense."

"None taken; you try harder."

"Are you staking a claim of interest?"

Joshua considered his brother's words. "We'll see."

He recognized that she was smart and tenacious, which alone made her very attractive to him. Of course, it didn't hurt that she was mighty fine-looking too. He only hoped that her confidence wasn't misplaced. If Thursday turned out to be a disaster, she probably wouldn't be staying.

Chapter 2

Colin smiled to himself as he pulled away from the ranch; unless he was very much mistaken, there was some chemistry bubbling between Ryden and his cousin, but he kept his observation to himself. There was so much to catch up on and they talked all of the way home.

"So, how are my favorite aunt and uncle?"

"Fine and working hard on the farm as usual. How about your mum and dad?"

"Oh, I expect they've changed a bit physically since you last saw them. Obviously, they're getting older, but they are well. They wanted to see you this evening, so they'll be popping over to the house later with my brothers."

"Save me! Tom and Harry were six- and eight-year-old little horrors the last time I saw them."

"Well, they are twenty- and twenty-four-year-old big horrors now." He laughed. "What about the Terrible Twosome?" Colin was referring to Rachael's older twin brothers.

"At the moment, they're in Aberdeen, Scotland, working on the offshore oil rigs. I think they may decide to come back here, though. They've been thinking about it for a while."

"They aren't settled yet then?"

"No, they're still a bit wild, but I think Meadow Ridge County might be the place for them. I'm not certain, but I suspect they want a lifestyle like yours."

Rachael hadn't been able to make it to Colin's wedding, so he told her about his family. Susan was a teacher at the local primary school and Mark owned an air courier company. They lived in town, conveniently located near Colin's practice, the school, and the airport. He marvelled to himself at his good fortune; the relationship was working even better than they had expected. He and his best friend loved their wife; they all complemented each other. Susan was the sweetest woman he had ever known, and she gave so much of herself that he felt almost humbled. He couldn't get enough of her and had been worried, at the beginning of the relationship, that he and Mark would be too much for her. It was an unfounded concern. She was a siren in the sack and demanded as much as they could give. They were lucky guys, no doubt about it.

"The relationship we have is working out really well. If your brothers think that they want to share a woman, they could do worse than to come here. What about you? Are you looking for two hunky guys?"

"Me with two men? Well, I guess it would depend on the guys, but I can't see it. I haven't found one Mr. Right yet, nevermind two."

When they arrived at Colin's home, both Mark and Susan dashed out to meet her.

"We rushed home from work as soon as we could. Welcome back, Rachael." Susan gave her a big hug.

"Save some for me, babe," Mark said, tackling Rachael away from his wife.

"It's great to finally meet you both. I feel like I know you already."

Colin patted his friend on the back and gave their wife a squeeze. "Go inside, ladies. We'll get the bags."

* * * *

Rachael instantly liked Mark and Susan. They were fun and easy to get along with. She noticed how often the guys touched their wife with fleeting kisses and caresses unconsciously given. It was clear to

Rachael that Susan adored both of her husbands. The woman positively glowed. Powered by a whole lot of loving, Rachael observed.

They chatted for a while before Rachael confessed that she desperately needed a power nap and a shower. The guys had already put her bags in the room that she would be using, and Susan showed her the layout of the place.

"There's a small en suite bathroom off your room, but if you want a super soak then use the master bathroom."

"Wow, I'm in heaven," Rachael exclaimed when Susan opened the door onto a huge bathroom. There was a massive tub and a shower cubicle obviously designed to accommodate at least three adults.

That evening, Rachael was hugged and fussed over more than she could ever remember. Colin hadn't been kidding about his brothers. They were tall, strapping young men but were still naughty boys at heart. Tom had picked her up and given her a big, bouncy bear hug before passing her to Harry without her legs even touching the ground. Her uncle had to choke back tears when Rachael showed him the short video that her mother had made for him.

"It's been too long," he said, smiling with wobbly lips. "I've missed my big sister."

"She misses you, too, Uncle Earl. It's hard for them to take long holidays and leave the farm, but Dad's thinking about selling up. Maybe they'll have more time then."

They all realized that Rachael was jetlagged, even though she tried desperately to stifle the yawns. Excitement had kept her lively, but toward ten thirty she was starting to wilt. They said good night and made her promise to come for supper the next evening. She thanked Colin, Mark, and Susan for their hospitality and padded off to bed. Her last conscious thought concerned a certain rancher with dark hair and malamute eyes.

* * * *

Rachael spent the next few days getting reacquainted with Ridge Water, the people, and her family. She vaguely remembered some of the folks who Colin introduced her to, others not at all. Everyone was very welcoming, though, and treated her like a long-lost relative. Her parents and grandparents had obviously been very popular people.

She quickly realized that staying in Colin's spare room could only be a very temporary arrangement. Even after just two days, she was beginning to feel voyeuristic and not just a little jealous. The sooner she got on with fixing up her grandma's old cabin the better. Grandma's cabin, which was known locally as Flora's Place, was about twenty minutes out of town. Family tradition demanded that the oldest daughter inherit the property. It had been left to Rachael's mother many years ago, who in turn had signed it over to Rachael on her twenty-first birthday. Colin had been using it occasionally and keeping an eye on the place. He took Rachael to see it when she suggested she might want to live there.

The cabin sat in twenty acres of woodland that had a stream running through it. It was old, but had been upgraded in a manner sympathetic to the original design. Instead of small pokey windows, it had glass doors that opened onto a veranda. There was a large combined kitchen-dining-living area, open to the rafters, spacious and light. There was a sleeping-storage area in half of the rafters, and the main bedroom was situated at one end of the cabin. It contained a big, beautiful four-poster bed that had been there as long as anyone could remember. Unfortunately, the mattress was almost as old and needed replacing. A modern bathroom had been tacked on at the back of the cabin and was accessible through a small hallway leading off the main room and to the back door. It was in need of a little sprucing up, but she loved it, especially the location amid the trees and next to flowing water.

Over the next few days, she worked tidying up the cabin. She found the physical activity to be therapeutic and let her thoughts wander over the landscape of her life. She'd had a good run of it so far and didn't take it for granted. Her parents had provided a happy, stable home, and she loved her family. She thought about Shannon O'Reilly, her Irish best friend and ardent environmentalist. They'd met at university and forged a friendship that Rachael knew would stand the distance and time apart. She was confident that when they met up again they would easily pick up where they left off. Shannon travelled, sometimes internationally, advising on projects, improvement schemes, and management of the environment. She seemed to thrive on meeting new challenges. Seeing this had galvanized Rachael into action.

Despite her relatively content life, she hadn't been too successful on the romantic front. Rachael had always been a little disappointed that she easily got her own way and that men tended to defer to her. As a consequence, she became bored quickly. In all honesty, no challenge for dominance had led to a lack of interest. She hadn't found a man who made her feel fulfilled, particularly in bed. She had briefly considered being more promiscuous; it would improve the odds of finding someone more sexually compatible, but she'd dismissed the idea because it seemed shallow and she wanted a connection with her partner.

She had dark fantasies which ranged from being forced into sexual submission to being the one doing the dominating. It confused her. In the rational light of day, such desires seemed at best kinky, and at worst base and perverse. She couldn't deny it to herself but kept these urges locked up and had never met anyone she could trust with the key.

She mused that it would be nice to have another person whom she could occasionally rely on to come home after a day of being in charge at work and hand over the reins, to not to have to make all the decisions all of the time. Her thoughts meandered in the direction of Joshua Ryden. She couldn't imagine anyone bossing him around. What was going on there, with the phenomenal level of attraction she'd experienced? She sighed. The problem was that she didn't know what she wanted. What was the missing ingredient? Maybe Joshua Ryden had it, or perhaps that was just a recipe for disaster.

When Thursday came around, she was almost as anxious to see him as she was to prove herself to be a good vet. Colin and Rachael drove out to Sweet Water Ranch in the morning with the equipment. Mark had ensured that the probe had been air couriered in time for the job. They parked near the paddock where the bull was tied to a post. James and Joshua were both leaning against the wooden fence, waiting as she exited the truck. They looked too gorgeous to be legal, but it was the dark-haired, bigger man who attracted her. She noticed his clenched jaw and wondered if he was more worried than she was.

Taking off the light jacket that she had worn against the early morning chill, she noticed about twenty men lined up along the paddock fence, all looking her way. Colin explained that the bush telegraph had been working well. Word of the procedure had gotten around, and a few of the neighboring cattlemen and nearly all of the Sweet Water ranch hands wanted to watch.

Slightly annoyed at the unexpectedly large audience, she nevertheless smiled and nodded in their direction, and then stretched and warmed up the muscles on her arms, neck, and shoulders in preparation for the work ahead.

After donning their white coats, Rachael and Colin walked over to Joshua, James, and George, the ranch foreman. She swept her gaze across them all before focusing on Joshua.

"Do they want popcorn and sodas?" She jerked her head in the direction of the men.

"It's not a procedure we've used before. They're curious. A few neighbors want to see how this technique works," Joshua said. "Does it bother you?"

Not as much as you do. "No, just as long as they're quiet and don't disturb our boy here."

As she walked into the paddock, she said good morning to the men, and they each raised a hat and mumbled, "Morning," back. Aware that she was under close observation, she turned to the foreman and began issuing instructions.

First, Rachael checked the ground to make sure that it was flat and that the bull would have a good footing. Then, she inspected the pen to ensure it was as she'd specified. She had the foreman lead the bull into it and fit bars behind so that the animal was restrained and couldn't move either side to side or back and forth. When this was done, she donned a plastic sleeve and safety glasses and commenced with an internal examination of the bull's organs.

With her arm deep inside the big animal, Rachael gently massaged and spoke soothingly to help it relax. Out of the corner of her eye, she noticed a lot of shifting feet and fidgeting at the fence. Because the bull was so big, she had ordered the largest rectal probe. Any quiet conversation between the men stopped completely as she slowly inserted it. They were watching with rapt interest. She softly described how she was commencing stimulation on the lowest power level and that a steady rhythm was required by turning the probe on and off every few seconds. Slowly, she increased the power level, explaining that soon the penis would protrude and seminal fluid would appear. From that point on, it was simply a case of rapidly increasing the power until the point of ejaculation, when Colin would collect the sample. The procedure went perfectly to plan without a hitch.

* * * *

"Well, I'll be damned," someone muttered.

She carefully removed the probe and eyed it thoughtfully for a few seconds before looking pointedly at Joshua and James.

"Judging by that look, I don't think she's happy about the size of the audience." James winced.

"She'll get over it," Joshua replied.

"Well, I'd say she aced the test." James grinned.

At first, Joshua didn't speak, which was unusual for him when it concerned anything about the ranch.

"It—she—was satisfactory," he finally said. "That's why she won't be annoyed. It will be good for her reputation."

Truth be told, he was very impressed and not just a little relieved by her competence and the commanding, yet calm and respectful, way she'd directed his men. He had suffered all morning from the warring feelings of apprehension and excitement. He'd wanted her to do well because he wanted to see her again, but his bull was an expensive animal and there were a lot of people watching.

James chuckled. "I don't think there is a more envied critter in the whole of Texas than that bull today. Satisfactory doesn't cut it."

"She was effective."

"Hell yeah, but I won't go on because I'll sound like a pervert." He affectionately punched his brother's arm.

"You *are* a pervert." Joshua snorted. "I'm checking the bull."

"It takes one to know one," James called after him.

* * * *

Rachael was aware of the imposing figure of Joshua Ryden strolling toward her as she stripped off the arm glove, turning it inside out in the process, and placed it in her bag. Her heart thumped in her chest, her cheeks flushed, her palms became cold, her mouth watered, and butterflies fluttered in her stomach. Jesus, she'd better pull herself together and concentrate on the bull and business rather than contend with the physical reactions that merely this guy's proximity seemed to create.

"He responded well to the procedure. He'll just need to rest in a quiet place for a short while." She spoke clearly and slowly, focusing on breathing normally and trying not to look like a silly schoolgirl or a sex-starved spinster.

"You give a good demonstration. It was well done. I'll take him to the barn. I think that a few people want to speak to you." He indicated to the men leaning against the paddock fence.

Rachael nodded, trying to appear natural and nonchalant, but was unable to resist looking up into those piercing blue eyes. They held each other's gaze for much longer than necessary. *Bloody hell, get away. Too intense. Move, damn it!* She spun on her heel and walked quickly in the direction of the other men, when all she really wanted to do was rub herself all over Joshua Ryden's big, hard body and give him a demonstration of an altogether different kind.

Realizing the ranchers were potential clients, she quickly pulled herself together and plastered a friendly, professional smile on her face.

"Are there any questions, gentlemen?"

The audience had some pertinent questions to ask her. For example, what would happen if the bull became agitated? Rachael explained clearly that if the bull was to become fretful, the stimulation must be stopped and the power increased at a more gradual pace. Most of the men wanted to introduce themselves, and more than one hinted about the county dance planned for the coming Saturday night. It was a good hour later before she finished. All the time, she had been aware of Joshua keeping his distance, talking to the other men, occasionally glancing her way. When everyone had left, she strolled over to Colin and James, who patted her on the back just like her brothers used to.

"Good job. Fancy a date?" James said, wiggling his eyebrows.

"You really are incorrigible, aren't you?" She feigned shock and then laughed.

"Only when I try, but maybe you prefer your men like your coffee? Speaking of which, would you like a cup?"

"I really need to get back to town. I have a long list of things," she paused for a moment completely losing focus, "to do, but maybe just a quick one."

"A quickie coming up—although it's not my normal style." James grinned.

His little joke was lost on her because she was totally distracted by the scene unfolding behind him. Joshua was standing by the outside wash stand, stripping off his shirt.

James looked over his shoulder and then back at Rachael with an amused expression.

He cleared his throat and barely kept the chuckle out of his voice as he muttered, "I'll just be a minute then." He headed to the house.

Captivated, Rachael watched as Joshua splashed water over his face and torso. *Bloody hell, he is a spectacular example of a man.* He looked strong and hard with muscles clearly defined on his shoulders and back. She shook her head to clear her thoughts. It was not professional to get distracted on the job by a client. James was cute and almost indecently good-looking, but Joshua attracted her like a moth to a flame. She couldn't bring herself to look away when he turned around, drying himself with a towel. Lord above, his front was even better, with a solid chest, clearly defined abs and a V-shaped slab of taut muscle disappearing into his jeans. She quickly dropped her eyes and then furtively looked at Colin.

"Careful cuz, Josh is not a vanilla kind of guy, if you get my drift."

Was he talking about kinky sex? Oh, sweet Mary, the very thought excited her, and she felt her panties dampen. "Well, I sure as hell don't expect him to be a tutti-frutti."

* * * *

Joshua wondered what Rachael had said to make Colin bark out a laugh. She had intelligence and sass, and he found it to be a potent combination. He was aware that she was watching him. Her presence was like gravity, constantly exerting an influence, pulling him to her. He strode over, shrugging on his shirt.

Just then Colin's cell phone rang, and he turned away to answer it.

"I hope that you won't object if I work with Colin at the ranch when needed?" Rachael looked a little flustered.

When needed? Right now, on all fours. "No, I don't mind, you're...good enough." Joshua said, again remembering the conversation in his UV.

His voice sounded strained, even to his own ears, and he was almost gnashing his teeth. *What the hell?* Within seconds of him being near her, his cock had become engorged, hard and ready. He shifted his position and held his hat in front of his groin to hide his evident arousal.

Colin finished the call. "That was John Greenhall on the phone. He has a problem with one of his horses. I don't need you with me, but as it's not far from here. I'll go directly. I'm sorry, Rach, but you'll have to put off your home improvements until later."

Joshua immediately said, "I'll give Rachael a ride if she wants. I'm headed into town anyway." Yeah, he'd dearly love to give her the ride of her life.

Rachael blushed as if she had read his mind. "Okay," she nearly croaked.

"Thanks. I'd better have a rain check on that coffee and get right on over there." Colin gave her a quick hug. "You were great today." He got into his truck and, after a quick glance at Joshua, added, "Remember what I said. I'll see you at home later."

Joshua wondered just what Colin had said. He couldn't think how the topic of his sexual preferences would have arisen but, now that Colin was gone, she looked a little distracted and flustered. She seemed to be trying to avoid looking at him. He noted how she rubbed her palms against her thighs, and wished that it were his hands there instead. She breathed deeply and her nostrils flared. He guessed that he was affecting her as much as she was affecting him.

"Are you all right?"

"I, er, yes," she squeaked. "I'm just going to cool down and freshen up."

She quickly dodged past him and headed to the washstand. After frantically peeling off her white coat, she thrust her hands into the running cold water and vigorously splashed her face and chest. She now glowed with vitality rather than embarrassment as she patted herself dry with a towel from her bag.

As before, Joshua was struck by her natural beauty. She wasn't wearing makeup and her skin looked great. The body-hugging vest she was wearing molded itself to her firm breasts. He unconsciously licked his lips. He wanted this woman—wanted to touch every inch of her and taste her skin, her lips, and her pussy. Hell, the prisoner in his pants wanted out now, and it was darn uncomfortable. He slammed his hat on his head and buttoned up his shirt, leaving it hanging loose to hide the obvious bulge in his jeans.

James appeared with coffee. "Where's Colin?"

"He has a job over at John Greenhall's place. I'll take Rachael on my way into town."

"You will?" smirked James.

"Home. I'll take her home," he quickly clarified, sounding flustered, which was a first. "Oh, for God's sake," he muttered with exasperation, more surprised by his own behavior than James was.

"Ahem, perhaps I should get a lift with you, too," James teased.

"No, you shouldn't," Joshua growled.

"Maybe you're right," James said, failing to hide a mischievous grin.

Rachael now appeared cooler and calmer as she sashayed over holding each end of the towel as it hung around her neck.

"Here's your coffee, Rachael. Strong, dark, and definitely not sweet."

James handed a coffee to her and one to Joshua. As he turned to get his own from the house, she flicked her towel, lightly catching him on the butt.

"Ow! Careful, darlin', you'll give me ideas."

"Ideas? What a novel experience for you."

He clutched his chest. "You wound me with your sharp wit, but now I know you'll be thinking about it."

"For goodness' sake, don't you ever stop?" Joshua sighed.

When James was about to answer, Joshua interrupted. "It was a rhetorical question, I know you don't."

* * * *

After they had finished their drinks, Joshua and Rachael left in the same vehicle she'd arrived in four days ago. Trying to put the maximum possible distance between them, she positioned herself on the far side of the cab next to the door. The analytical side of her mind recognised that natural animal instinct was making her wary. He was a prime male in close proximity to a fertile and, if she were honest, receptive female. *Gosh, I can't stop thinking like a vet. It's pathetic.*

They drove for a while in silence. The cab, which at first had seemed so spacious, now felt confining. She could see, hear, and smell him. If she wanted to—and she did—she could touch and taste him. But there was something else, a sixth sense maybe, operating on another level. Her chest swelled as she breathed deeply, her nostrils flared when she caught a slight waft of his masculine scent, and her body sang in recognition of a primeval melody that her mind refused to acknowledge: special, compatible, potential mate. Of course, it could just be the "pheromone fairies" out to trick her into doing something rash. Already she felt that her panties were damp just from being so close to him. She was finding it difficult not to fidget and wriggle.

* * * *

As he slowed the truck for the cattle grid at the border of the property, Joshua briefly glanced at Rachael. She didn't look comfortable, but then neither was he with a raging hard-on straining to get out of his jeans and say hello. Damn but his cock was turning into a demanding dictator. Attempting to ease the tension building between them, he asked Rachael about her immediate plans.

"So you're fixing up Flora's Place to move into?"

"Yes," she explained. "Colin, Mark, and Susan are great, but I think I'm cramping their style, if you know what I mean."

"Um, I can imagine, but what about your style?"

"Nothing to cramp." She sighed and shrugged.

"I find that hard to believe."

"Well, I did have a boyfriend, but it ended three months ago."

No boyfriend, good.

"You seem to enjoy flirting with my brother." There, he'd said it, the thing that bothered him.

"Yes, but you know what they say about flirting don't you? Flirtation is just tension without the intention," she quoted.

Clever, and perhaps she doesn't fancy my brother.

"That's probably why you don't flirt, Joshua."

"What do you mean?" He was intrigued by her observation.

"I doubt you do anything without intention."

She was right.

Suddenly he swerved the UV off the road and brought it to an abrupt halt behind a clump of thick bushes. In one fluid quick move, he slapped both seat belts open and dragged her across his lap.

"W–What are—"

"What am I doing? I want you in my bed. I've thought of little else since I met you, but I can't wait," he ground out.

Raw instinct pushed all thoughts from his mind other than to take this woman and to screw her senseless. With an arm under her, he roughly pulled her to him and crushed his mouth down on hers. It wasn't a gentle kiss but a fierce possessive assault on her lips that claimed her mouth, allowed no refusal.

At first, she weakly attempted to resist, with a protest muffled by his kiss. "You're a client. This is not professional."

"Who cares?" He knew in the back of his mind that he should, but the aching need to have her was simply too strong.

He pressed harder and she responded by relaxing her jaw and parting her lips. It was sheer bliss as she willingly received him and they shared their first kiss, full of passion and promise for things destined to come. His tongue slipped into the warm wet confines of her mouth, then thrust deeper, duelling with hers. She snaked her arms up around his neck and ran her fingers through his hair. He could sense her fevered desire. It matched his own.

He moved his free hand under her T-shirt, pushing it over her breasts.

"Front fastener," she said throatily.

"Smart girl."

He deftly unclipped her bra and released her breasts, beautiful, ample pale globes topped with pretty, candy-pink nipples. His cock would fit nicely between them, and that image flitted in his mind as he buried his face and sucked hard on each pert bud while he undid the button and zipper of her jeans. He slid his hand under the scrap of lace that masqueraded as underwear, down over her smooth, partially shaved mound, and felt the moist evidence of her arousal. He gently skimmed his middle finger and thumb over her wet pussy lips and then pressed on her clit in a circular motion.

"Oh, God, that feels so good," she gasped as she tilted her hips and parted her legs more.

He responded to her unspoken invitation and plunged his thick finger into her creaming cunt. Her eyes widened as she watched him slowly remove his hand and put the finger to his mouth.

"Delicious."

She tasted exquisite. He knew that he would enjoy lapping at her pussy when she was more comfortable and he could take his time, but not now. He returned his hand to between her legs and reinserted his finger. She clenched around it as he slowly moved his hand back and forth, returning pressure on her swollen clit with his thumb.

She tugged on his hair to bring his lips in contact with hers again to be devoured by a ravenous kiss. He moaned into her mouth as she writhed on his lap. Her hip pressed against the outline of his hard length straining against the confines of his jeans. She squirmed more and ground against him, and he matched her rhythm with his hand. It was her turn to moan.

He kissed and nipped his way down her throat to her breasts and sucked on her tits again, alternating between them, gently biting and pulling the hard, protruding nipples. He stopped playing with her breasts for a moment to look into her dark brown eyes. The pupils were dilated with desire, and he knew that he could lose himself in the depths of that gaze.

She slowly closed her eyes and tipped her head back, exposing her throat and pushing her breasts upward. It was both a wanton and submissive gesture, which ignited his passion further. He returned his mouth to her nipple and flicked and sucked more forcefully. The sensation began like the small tremors preceding a major earthquake. Her clit was the epicenter, and he felt the shock waves languidly radiating outwards through her body. She stiffened and jerked.

"Joshua, I'm coming," she cried out as her channel gripped and undulated around this finger, flooding his hand with her juices.

He felt a sense of urgency like never before. It screamed at him to take her any which way, to take her now. He removed his hand and clawed at her clothes, yanking her jeans down and off. Flinging the door open, he half dragged her through. She stumbled as her feet hit the ground for a moment before being lifted up against the side of the UV.

"Rachael, if you don't want this, say so now," he said with barely restrained lust as he tore open his jeans enough to release his huge cock.

Ten and a half inches of ridged, wide shaft sprang out.

* * * *

Want it? She needed it, craved it, and was desperate for it. Moments ago the sensations emanating from her breasts and between her legs had become uncontainable. Shockwaves had crashed up her spine to her brain and down her legs to her toes as she'd climaxed hard. Her pussy now begged for something bigger than his finger to clasp and squeeze around and as luck would have it...

She wrapped her legs around him and ground against him.

"Don't," she pleaded with a moan.

He tensed

"Don't," she kissed him, "stop."

"Is that a yes or a no?" he said in frustration.

"It's a yes, damn it. Don't stop."

One arm gripped her ass, holding her off the floor, while the other ripped off her panties and positioned the head of his glistening cock against her plump swollen nether lips. For a second, he hesitated, and then he groaned her name as he pushed into her, forging through warm, tight, moist muscle.

"Oh, Jesus, yes," he said.

He filled her completely, stretching her cunt to an almost painful limit. Crying out, she sank her teeth into the shirt on his shoulder to muffle her scream. For a moment he stopped, giving her time to adjust, then slowly began to pump into her.

Her passion raged like a wildfire on parched land. She made soft mewing noises and gasps, urging him on. He didn't hold back for long and picked up the pace. He thrust into her faster, harder, and deeper. She could feel the friction of his thick, hard length along the uneven muscular surface of her tightly fisted channel, slick with her juices, as he repeatedly plunged forward and pulled back.

She heard him grunting with each thrust. "Can't—last—much—longer."

"You don't have to," she cried as another climax caused her to jerk and squeeze her legs around him.

She leaned back against the vehicle and spread her arms out in abandonment as he pushed against her. She was helpless. He dictated the pace, and it was perfect. He began to pump his hips faster. She clenched her inner muscles and shuddered and bucked as her orgasm continued to blaze through her. She howled his name as her cunt undulated, milking his cock, causing him to cry out.

"Oh, fuck yes. That's right, take it all," he demanded as he violently shot his load deep inside her.

Panting, they held each other closely as the aftershocks subsided. Slowly, he lifted her off him and loosened his hold. She slid down his body to stand on uncertain legs, wobbly like a newborn colt, but glad that he still held and supported her weight. He tilted her face up and bent down to kiss her while caressing her back.

He was about to speak when she became aware of something sticky seeping down her thigh. Realization hit her like a bucket of cold water.

"Damn, we didn't use a condom. I've never done that before. Stupid, stupid girl," she said, disgusted with herself and annoyed with him.

"Me, neither. I'm sorry. I wasn't thinking." He sounded shocked.

"You were thinking, all right, just not with your brain."

He looked taken aback. "If it's any consolation, I had an annual medical a month ago and I'm clear of any STDs. What about you?"

"I don't sleep around. I also had a medical before coming here. All clear."

"So there's no problem then, except," he paused, eyes widening, "what about contraception?"

"I had a hormone implant. I'm a belt-and-braces kind of girl. I had planned to get it removed. Thank goodness I didn't. I'm hopefully good for another three months or so."

He tenderly lowered his forehead to hers. "So we're good, then?" he sighed in relief.

"Yes...no! I can't believe I behaved so irresponsibly."

"Contraception is a joint responsibility. If it's any consolation, I feel the same way. I just lost control. It doesn't happen often, Rachael, but I've got to say, it felt—*you* felt amazing."

She glared at him for making her a quick fuck by the side of the road, but then softened it to a small smile because she couldn't regret the spontaneous, amazing sex.

"It felt great for me, too, but, Josh, I don't know much about you and you know next to nothing about me."

"I know there's something between us, Rachael."

She looked pointedly down at his semi-erect cock. "You don't say."

But she knew he was right. There was some kind of connection between them. When she had bought her small house in England two years ago, she had known as soon as she saw the front door that she would want it. It was the same certainty with Joshua Ryden. That didn't mean it couldn't all end horribly and in tears. She got dressed without her panties, which were unsalvageable, and he rearranged his clothes. He tenderly pulled her to him and kissed the top of her head before he helped her into the cab.

They didn't speak much for the rest of the journey, both deep within their own thoughts.

* * * *

"Thanks for the ride." She gave a little quirky grin as they arrived at Colin's home.

"My pleasure," he said seriously. "I want to see you again."

"Yes, but give me a few days. A lot has happened to me in a short space of time. I think I need to get my bearings."

"Okay. I'll call you."

He got out of the truck and opened the door for her. As he helped her down, his big hands lingered on her neat waist. Her breathing seemed shallower as she stared at him with chocolate brown eyes. Already he wanted her again. Her gaze lowered slowly to his crotch and the very obvious large, uncomfortable-looking bulge that nestled there. She raised her eyebrows in a look he interpreted as surprise and possibly admiration. He wasn't a braggart, but he knew that he packed an impressive weapon—more of a bazooka than a love gun. She stepped forward and lightly rubbed against him.

"Until then," she murmured, then turned and walked away.

It took all his resolve not to throw her over his shoulder and carry her off to the nearest hotel. Unfortunately, or perhaps fortunately, he didn't have the time because he had to pick his sister up from the airport. He understood that Rachael needed time to process what had happened. Hell, they both did. He had never had such a strong compulsion to fuck anyone like that before. He hadn't wanted it to end. The need to take her completely—to have her come around his cock as he came inside her—had been fierce. So much so that he had been stupid enough to forget to use a condom, something that had never happened before. The pleasure of warm, wet flesh to flesh contact while riding her bareback made all other experiences pale in comparison.

There was something about her that called to him, and his instinct was to hunt it down. Joshua knew that he had to be more patient. He didn't want to scare Rachael off. If only she guessed his thoughts about what he would like to do to her. Would she run from him and never want to see him again? He wanted to be honest about his desires. Otherwise, it would be unfair to them both. He remembered her submitting to his control today, so perhaps she wasn't averse to a bit of domination in the bedroom. He hoped he'd find out soon enough.

Chapter 3

Rachael was glad that no one was home when she entered the house. She needed to clean herself up and time to absorb what had just happened. A long, hot shower would help, although she was reluctant to wash his scent away. The sex had been incredible. She had the sneaking suspicion that she'd been short changed in the past. Now she finally knew what it was to be "taken" by a real man, and the corporeal knowledge of it had an addictive quality, stimulating feel-good endorphins—infusing her blood, her flesh, and her very bones with desire, and leaving her desperate for more. Jesus, her mouth watered and she was short of breath just thinking about him. It wouldn't do, no, not at all. She'd better pull herself together before she unravelled completely. *I can't just fall for the first attractive man I've met here. He can't be "the one," can he?* It all seemed so unlikely, yet a simple word tugged on the treads of her tangled thoughts—fate.

She was determined to keep busy to avoid the warring cycles of thoughts developing—one a vicious circle that always ended in disappointment and her professional reputation in tatters, the other a virtuous one leading to satisfaction and happily ever after. It was uncomfortable and distracting and better not to be thought about at all. Yes, she should be able ignore her turbulent emotions—she was half-English after all.

After a quick lunch, armed with the materials that she had just purchased from the local hardware store, she headed to her cabin. She was going to paint the main room a bright sunshine yellow—Summer Memory it said on the tin. She hoped it would lighten her mood and take her mind off things. She docked her iPod into the small but powerful sound system that she had brought with her from England and chose her exercise playlist. The fast, energetic music lifted her spirits, and she sang along as she got to work cleaning the walls and taping areas to be kept paint-free.

By late afternoon, she was finishing the first coat of paint and realized that she would need another ten liters. She resolved to finish the job the next morning. Just before she was about to leave, the department store called and asked if she would be at the cabin around noon tomorrow to receive the king-size mattress she had ordered the day before. Great. With any luck, she would spend Saturday night in her new home, in her grandma's four-poster fairytale bed.

When she arrived at her cousin's house, Susan and Colin were there. Mark was making an air delivery to a more remote ranch and would be home later.

"Hey, guys, you'll be glad to know that you'll have the house to yourselves after tomorrow night. I'm moving into Flora's Place on Saturday."

"Now, you know we love having you here, I'll miss the female company," Susan said kindly. "You are still coming to the county dance with us on Saturday night at the high school, aren't you? It's a real community event. Everyone goes."

"Yeah, sure, I wouldn't miss it. Sounds fun."

"Great. Because both my men love to dance, and it can get pretty tiring. I'll need some support." She giggled.

"I think our Rachael will be kept busy enough. She had plenty attention today at the ranch."

You have no idea. She couldn't prevent her blushing.

"They'll be more than one cowboy hoping for a turn around the dance floor," Colin continued.

"What? I've never Texan two-stepped in my life. I'm more of a hip-hop sort of girl."

"Have you ever line danced?" Susan asked.

"No, but I'm willing to try, just please don't make me dance to 'Achy Breaky Heart.'" She laughed.

"The annual dance is for all of the community, so the music is varied. Country is a firm favorite, but when the live band isn't playing, the DJ makes sure there's something for everyone." Susan grinned. "And, anyway, I happen to like a bit of Billy Ray."

"Yes, but which bit?" Rachael teased.

* * * *

The next morning, bright and early, Rachael headed to the hardware store to get more Summer Memory. As she walked to her nearly new Jeep, she noticed a ruckus between a man and young woman in the parking lot. The man was half in the truck holding onto the woman's wrist, and she appeared to be trying to pull away. Rachael hesitated for a moment, then shouted. "Oi! You, there, are you okay?"

The man quickly let go, sat back in the truck, and raced off, leaving the woman rubbing her wrist.

Rachael trotted over and repeated, "Are you okay? Do you need any help?"

"N—no thanks. I'm fine, just a bit shook up."

The woman didn't look fine. Rachael figured that she had an hour to spare. The mattress was arriving at noon and it was now only nine thirty. "Well, I'm sort of new in town and I was thinking of getting a coffee. Want you join me? I'm Rachael."

"Thanks, Rachael. My name's Janet." They shook hands. "I think I will join you. I could do with a bit of female company right about now."

Janet suggested a small coffee shop across the street, and they headed to it. As they both ordered a cappuccino, Rachael could see that Janet looked agitated, so she waited for her to speak first.

"That guy you saw with me is such a jerk. His name is Roy Crossling, and he won't take no for an answer. He keeps pestering me."

"It looked a lot more than pestering, if you don't mind me saying."

Janet was quiet for a moment, and then, like a burst dam, the words flooded out. "Oh, God, it's partly my fault. I should have nipped it in the bud early on, but somehow, before I realized, it got much worse. I only arrived home from college yesterday, and already he's bothering me. I'm worried because, if my brothers find out, they'll be angry with me for not telling them sooner. It'll end in trouble, and I don't know what to do." She looked as if she was about to cry. "It started a year ago when he wanted to date me, and I told him nicely that I wasn't interested. It just didn't seem to register with him. He first started making crude comments, you know, about my butt or my boobs. Then, as I ignored him, he started 'accidentally' brushing up against me, but when I complained, he just laughed. Today, he wanted me to go for a ride in this car and actually tried to pull me in. What am I going to do? It's getting to the stage that I don't want to come home from college or be out alone!"

Rachael put her hand on Janet's arm and squeezed. "Listen to me, it's not your fault. Sometimes things creep up on you." She paused for a moment, thinking how to explain it. "It's the boiling-frog scenario."

Janet looked up, puzzled.

"You see, research has shown that if you put a frog into a pan of hot water it will immediately jump out. But, if you put the frog into cool water and then slowly heat the water up, the frog won't jump out, but will stay in the water as it boils."

"That's horrible."

"Yes, but do you get the point? If this guy had tried to drag you into his car at the beginning, you would have done something about it straight away. Because he started off with small things and then gradually worsened, you haven't acted. You're not to blame. It's a natural reaction, but you have to ask yourself if you really want to get to boiling point."

"No. Wow, Rachael, when you say it like that I feel a whole lot better. I felt ashamed for not handling it, but really I should just be angry at Roy."

"Yes, so what will you do?"

"I'll tell my brothers." She looked relieved and happier. "Say, it's the county dance tomorrow night. Are you going? You could come with us if you haven't other plans."

"Thanks, that's a sweet offer, but I am going with my cousin, Colin Farley, the vet. I'll see you there, though."

"I know Colin fairly well." A look of recognition crossed her face, "Oh, you're *that* Rachael. I'm so glad to meet you, thanks again." She gave Rachael a hug and added with a mischievous grin, "I'll tell my brothers about the boiling frog. It may save me a lecture. I even feel slightly sorry for Roy because Josh and James will kick his ass."

Slightly stunned, Rachael sipped her coffee while she considered the new information. Janet was Joshua and James's sister, and they were going to the dance tomorrow night.

"So you're at college?" she finally spoke.

"Yep, I'm in my last year at Texas A&M studying business, same as Josh did. It's becoming a family institution. James graduated with an engineering degree, and both our fathers studied there."

"Oh, you had two fathers? I didn't realize."

"They were the best." She looked and sounded sad. "Our mother and fathers died in a car crash eleven years ago. I was only ten, James was seventeen, and Josh was twenty-one. He dropped out of college to look after James and me. He completed the last few months of lectures and final exams two years later, but by then he'd already been successfully running the ranch and our other business concerns. They are both great brothers, but Josh has been so much more. He literally took on the role of our parents."

"That was such a lot of responsibility for one so young."

"I know, but he still treats me like a child. I'm a grown woman now, and he's so protective. It's a habit, I guess, but he needs to just relax a bit, enjoy himself and let others worry about stuff for a change."

"It's easy to fall into a particular pattern of behavior and hard to see when it's no longer relevant."

"You see, you understand. You have a good way with words, Rachael."

"Well, saying and doing are two different things. Maybe when you've finished college you could be more actively involved in the family business, and demonstrate that you are ready to take on some responsibility. The alternative is to do your own thing somewhere else."

"That's something to think about," she nodded.

Rachael took a last sip of her coffee. "I'm afraid I have to finish a few chores today and be at my home for a delivery. It was really nice meeting you, Janet. I'll see you tomorrow evening. Good luck with your brothers."

By the time she got to her car, Rachael had made a number of conclusions about the Rydens. They were from a ménage family, so she guessed that Joshua and James probably wanted the same thing. How disappointing, because she couldn't imagine being intimate with James. He was too much like both of her brothers. Joshua was controlling and dominant, but now she understood why. She had to admit she liked the way he was. It was sexy, but she wondered if he would he ever be prepared to occasionally relinquish control. "Now *that* I'd like to see," she said to herself and then sighed, resigned to the fact that it wasn't going to happen.

Rachael drove to the cabin and quickly applied the second coat of paint. She made certain that all the doors were wide open to air the rooms. The mattress arrived, and she asked the two delivery guys, Lance and Paul, to help her put the old one in the rafters. It would do temporarily for guests. She offered them a coffee, and they both looked disappointed that they didn't have the time. They had other deliveries to make, and as it was their own business, they couldn't afford to be slack on the job.

"Are you going to the dance tomorrow night?" Lance asked.

"Sure am. I'm told it's a must-do thing."

"Well, save a dance for us then, Rachael." They grinned as they headed out to their truck.

She smiled and waved good-bye, feeling flattered by the attention but nothing more.

Rachael had already purchased linens and a few other items to allow more permanent habitation. The bed looked sumptuous with crisp, white Egyptian cotton sheets, and she couldn't help having a bounce on it. The cabin smelled like new and looked bright and cheery yet cozy. It would make a good little home.

* * * *

For most of the next day, Rachael moved her few belongings from Colin's house, but left a suitcase of clothes there because she was going to get ready for the dance with Susan and she hadn't decided what she was going to wear. She arrived early that evening because Susan wanted help with her hair.

"What are you gonna wear tonight, honey?" Susan asked as Rachael used the curling irons on her long blonde hair.

"I'm not sure. What's the dress code?" Rachael had brought a few fancy dresses with her from England, but they seemed a bit formal for a county dance.

"Well, obviously, jeans if you've no imagination. You can't go wrong with jeans, but I bet you'd look great in those brown leather snakeskin pants I spied in your case."

"Yeah, they'll do if I can fit into them. I can dress them up a bit with a gold strappy top I have. What about you?"

"Jeans. I've no imagination." Susan laughed. "But I'll wear black ones and a sexy sequined top. I have to keep my men on their toes, you know."

Rachael showered, shaved, and plucked. She normally kept her pussy partially bare, with a tuft of fuzz for the sake of decency in the women's locker room, but tonight she shaved it completely. Often, she dressed in practical clothes and kept a professional exterior, so it was her erotic little secret. It made her feel sensual and naughty. Her hair took no time at all because it only did one style: a short, curly bob. She finished applying a little makeup and added some gold hoop earrings and a gold choker. To her surprise, the pants slid on fairly easily and didn't feel tight at all. There were days when she had to springboard into them. She reckoned it was all the running around getting the cabin ready, not to mention all the small worries associated with relocating.

She checked herself in the mirror and was pleased with what she saw. Rachael wasn't petite. She had a body built for work, but instead of trying to starve herself thin, she had embraced her inherent strength—toned up, got fit and built some muscle. She turned around and inspected the rear view. Her butt actually looked quite good. It would never be described as small, but a little junk in the trunk was fashionable these days, and the thin, soft leather hugged her curves and hinted at the firm body beneath.

Her shimmering gold top revealed toned, slightly muscular arms that she worked hard to get. It wasn't simply a matter of vanity. She had to be able to cope with the physical demands of working with livestock. The top clung in all the right places, emphasizing her firm chest and flat stomach. *It's only a county dance. He might not even be there.* She cautioned herself about thinking of Joshua. If he wanted to share her with his brother, then it would have to be over before it really began.

She headed to the living room where Colin and Mark were waiting.

"My, my, doesn't she look fine?" Mark sang.

"She does indeed. We'll be beating them off with a stick," Colin replied.

"Well, I must say that you gentlemen look very dashing, too."

"That's why I married them, only for their looks," Susan chirped as she sauntered into the room.

Colin, Mark, and Rachael turned to Susan, who looked radiant. Her long hair fell in soft waves around her shoulders and down her back. Both men appeared totally smitten and stood stock still regarding their wife, with love and desire stamped all over their faces.

Mark swallowed hard. "You look so beautiful, darlin'. Colin and I must be the luckiest guys alive."

Judging by the intense stares, Rachael guessed that some heated nonverbal communication was going on between the three of them.

"Don't even think about it. We've got a guest." Susan chuckled sexily and winked at her men. They groaned and rolled their eyes.

"Oh, cheers, I'd feel bad if I thought that you weren't going to be getting any later, but right now I'm Norma No-Mate, and I can't bring myself to feel sorry for both of you, so saddle up and let's go," Rachael ordered with a cheeky grin.

* * * *

The organizers had done a great job of converting the school gym into a dance hall. The theme was Moonlight and Roses, and a huge full moon, redolent of the real full moon outside, was projected onto one wall. Garlands of paper roses were everywhere and every woman entering received a real red rose.

Susan hadn't exaggerated when she had said the dance was aimed at the whole community. Rachael saw all sorts of people of varying ages. There were grandmas with blue rinsed hair, grungy teenagers, pretty schoolgirls, sexy ladies, goths, cool hip-hop dudes and cowboys. She even spied a gang of leather-clad bikers at one table.

Some popular dance music was playing, and people were already on the dance floor, including Tom and Harry, who had a girl suggestively sandwiched between them.

"I need to speak to those two about appropriate behavior. This is a family event. Excuse me." Colin rolled his eyes and headed onto the dance floor to collar his brothers.

Rachael and Susan found an empty table while Mark went to the bar.

"I'll fill you in on everyone I know and all the juicy gossip." Susan chuckled.

As she looked around, Rachael spotted the man who had hassled Janet. "Hey, tell me about that guy." She pointed him out to Susan.

"Roy Crossling? Local yahoo, more looks than brains and that's not saying much. His family owns property that borders yours and the Rydens. Why?"

"He was bothering a woman the other day."

"It wouldn't surprise me. His momma left him and his daddy years ago. Couldn't put up with the abuse anymore, so the rumor goes. That boy needs a talking to and then some."

"Well, he might get it tonight."

"Really? Tell all."

"I'll explain later. Right now, I need the bathroom."

Susan pointed her in the general direction of the ladies' room, and Rachael wove in and out of the tables to get to the far side of the gym. She recognized a few of the guys from the Sweet Water Ranch and smiled a greeting in passing. It took twenty minutes to get across the room as friendly folks she'd met over the past few days inquired after her—How she was settling in? Did she need any help? Would she like a drink? She briefly exchanged pleasantries and her smile was open and genuine, until she saw a line of women along a wall. *Typical. There's always a queue for the ladies, but I bet not for the gents. It's enough to give a girl penis envy.*

"Hey, I'm glad that you're here." Janet was standing near the end of the line and gave her a big hug.

Rachael couldn't resist making a quick sweep of the room. She didn't see Joshua or James and relaxed a bit.

"I am so grateful to you. I told my brothers everything. At first, they were a bit annoyed with me for not saying anything to them sooner, but I gave them your boiling frog explanation and they backed off a bit. Even Josh understood. I think you have gone up even further in his estimation, and, let me tell you, that guy is hard to please."

"I bet." Rachael muttered, pleased with the compliment but telling herself to lock her feelings down because it just couldn't go any further. Suddenly, she noticed that Janet had visibly stiffened.

"Well, hello, Jan, fancy seeing you here," someone with a menacing voice drawled. "You shouldn't stand in line. Why don't you come with me? Next door is free."

Rachael turned to see Roy Crossling leering at Janet.

"No, thank you. I can think of better offers than a trip to the toilets with you," Janet said with her head held high and only a slight tremble in her voice.

"Ah, come on, Jan, or do you think you're too good for me?" he sneered slowly.

"Well, I certainly do. You are not getting the message. She is not interested in you." Rachael punctuated the last four words.

"You're a nosy bitch, y'know that?" he said between gritted teeth.

"Not normally," she said pleasantly then sharply dropped her smile. "But I can make an exception for you. Now bugger off." She maintained eye contact as he straightened. The other women in the queue were starting to take notice of the exchange.

"What makes you think you can tell *me* what to do?" he snapped.

"It's a thing called freedom of speech, Roy. What you decide to do is another matter, but we really don't want a scene here tonight."

Thinking that she was backing down, he sneered, "You're all bluff, aren't ya, Miss Sperm Collector?"

"Gosh, Roy, is that the best you can do?" Rachael sadly shook her head. "I suggest you save your breath. You'll need it to blow up your date."

"What?" he spluttered.

Several of the listening women snickered.

"Hard of hearing, too? Even with my expertise and knowledge on the matter, what I can't understand is how, out of one hundred thousand sperm, *you* were the fastest?"

There was some laughter now. His face burned with anger and embarrassment.

"Are you making fun of me?"

"No, not at all, I prefer a challenge. Making fun of you would be like hunting a dairy cow with a high-powered rifle and scope."

"Why, I'm gonna—"

"Get your ass kicked in about ten seconds," Rachael interjected. She had just seen Joshua, James, and another heavily muscled man heading quickly toward them.

"What?"

"Five, four, three, two, one." Rachael sang the countdown.

Before Roy had time to make a getaway, a big hand clamped down on his shoulder.

"We want a word with you," James snarled in a menacing voice Rachael couldn't imagine belonging to him.

"Outside now," Joshua ordered, his tone was cold and brooked no resistance. They hustled Roy quickly out of a side door.

"Damn it, Mitch," Janet said to the guy who had arrived with her brothers. "You're the deputy. Shouldn't you go with them to make sure nothing too bad happens?"

Rachael's attention snapped back to the big guy standing close to Janet. He was about the same height as James and had to be one of the broadest men she'd ever met. She found it hard to see past his frame. He'd be a good guy to hide behind in a gunfight. To "serve and protect," all he would need to do was stand there.

"I'm off duty, so I'm giving them two minutes. Why didn't you come and tell me about Roy?" He stood in front of her with his fists and teeth clenched. "I'd finish him myself if he'd hurt you."

"You would?" Janet timidly asked.

"You know I would." His face softened.

"At the time, I felt that I was overreacting."

"Yeah, Josh said something about a boiling frog." He looked slightly puzzled. "I'd better go rescue Roy, though it irks me to do it."

Watching the deputy leave, Rachael raised an eyebrow at Janet.

"What?" she said all wide-eyed and innocent.

"I think the deputy's smitten and I think you don't mind."

"It's complicated," sighed Janet. "Mitch is a really great guy, and I think he likes me, but he always holds back. I'm not sure why, but I think he still sees me as a little girl." She snorted. "It's a common problem with the men in my life and it's very frustrating."

"I'm sorry I can't help. I'm no expert on men. They surprise me all the time."

By the time Rachael and Janet sat down at Susan's table, Mitch and Joshua had returned to the room and were obviously looking for them. Janet frantically waved them over.

"You weren't hurt, were you?"

"No. James took a few swipes, but Roy was no match for him. He was fairly riled up by whatever you said to him, Rachael." Joshua looked admiringly at her and sounded positively cheery. "I stayed on the sidelines watching just in case."

"That's not like you." Janet looked suspicious.

"I didn't trust myself to not go too far. Anyway, two against one isn't our style."

Isn't it? Rachael couldn't help seeing a double entendre.

"Where's Roy?" Janet asked.

"Probably limping home with his tail firmly between his legs. He won't bother you again, munchkin."

"Thanks, but don't call me that." Janet grumbled. "I'm not twelve anymore." She looked at both Joshua and Mitch.

"Where is James?" Rachael asked.

"Pursuing a woman with Luke, as usual."

Oh my God, they share with others as well. Astonished, Rachael took a long swig of her beer. Lost in dark thoughts, she hadn't noticed that the music had changed. The band was now playing a lively country number.

"Let's dance," said Janet as she bounced up.

Rachael could see people forming lines. "I've never line danced before, but I'll have a go," she said, hardly catching a breath as Janet and Susan dragged her on to the floor with Colin and Mark. Rachael noticed that Joshua stayed put, talking to Mitch but often glancing her way. The deputy seemed similarly distracted, watching Janet.

It was a lot of fun, and her mood lifted a little. She found herself giggling as she messed up the steps. Lance and Paul were standing behind her in a line and kept pretending that she was stomping on their toes. It was very funny, and Janet was laughing heartily. Toward the end of the song, despite the boys clowning around, she was getting it right. After another lively number, the music changed to a slow country tune. Lance and Paul stepped in closer, but before they could say anything, a strong arm snaked around her waist and pulled her back against a hard body.

"The lady's taken," a deep male voice rumbled.

There was no mistaking the possessive power in those three words. Lance and Paul hesitated briefly then good-naturedly backed away. Towering over her, Joshua bent his head to whisper in her ear.

"Dance with me."

It wasn't a request.

Rachael didn't know what to say. She thought that she should have been outraged at the assumption he made, but her traitorous body relaxed against his, and she knew the truth of his words: taken. Whatever pheromones this guy was packing would make millions if bottled. His scent was just too darn alluring and clouded her thoughts. Keeping her enclosed within one arm, he turned her around to face him.

"You look beautiful and sexy tonight. You supported my sister and made a fool of Crossling. You are the most attractive, desirable woman I have ever met. I know you wanted some time, but come home with me tonight."

She was aware of his arousal as he held her closely and led her around the dance floor. She certainly wasn't unaffected. At this rate, she'd need to buy panty liners in bulk. Despite her feelings, she knew that she had to put the brakes on.

"Listen, Josh, I want to be honest with you. I won't play with your feelings or come between you and your brother. I can't live the lifestyle you want." Saying those words was as easy as chewing glass.

He looked confused, as if he didn't understand what she was saying.

"What?"

"It's James." Rachael didn't know how else to explain.

She looked at his face and saw hurt and frustration in his eyes. He released her from his embrace and stepped back.

"I apologize. I didn't realize. I—I made a mistake."

He turned abruptly and walked away, leaving her alone on the dance floor. Rachael felt bereft. A sense of emptiness surged through her, and she almost stumbled as she slowly walked back to her seat.

"Are you okay? What the heck just happened?" Janet whispered, looking worried.

Rachael took a deep breath and decided to tell her everything, figuring she'd find out sooner or later anyway.

"I like James, I really do, but not in *that* way."

"What?" Janet spurted incredulously. She blinked hard a few times, quickly putting together the pieces of the train-wreck of a misunderstanding. "Oh, you have it all wrong. Josh doesn't share a woman with anyone. He's not the sharing type. If anything, he's the opposite. James wants the same lifestyle that our parents had, but because Josh doesn't, he's looking with his friend Luke for the right woman."

"But—but, I assumed…"

"Well, you know what they say about *assume*? It makes an *ass* out of *u* and *me*."

"Oh, God, what a disaster. No, scratch that, it's actually good news, isn't it? I'm a twit of the highest order. I need to set this straight."

"So you like Josh then?"

"I fancy the pants off him. I'm just cautious, you know? I've been here such a short time, and I've still to get myself established both personally and professionally."

Janet smiled. "I think you'd be great together. He needs a strong woman."

Just then Mitch approached them. He maintained a concerned expression but failed to fully hide his delight.

"Er, I've just spoken to Josh on the phone. He asked me to take you home, Janet. What's up?"

"A misunderstanding, but it'll get sorted out. Can you take me soon?"

Mitch stared at her longingly. "Sure."

"You coming, Rachael?"

"Can you give me a lift to Colin's house? My Jeep's there, and I think I'll go home. Josh may not be in the mood to see me when he gets back to the ranch, and I want to think things through."

Feigning a headache to Susan and the guys, but suspecting that she was fooling no one, she headed out of the building with Janet and Mitch. When they pulled up next to Rachael's Jeep, she turned to Janet. "Tell him I'm sorry that I jumped to conclusions. Thanks for the lift, Mitch."

She waved good-bye as they drove away, wishing that she were going with them. Rachael wanted to set things straight, but there really wasn't a relationship yet. Rushing headlong to the ranch might not be the best move even though that was exactly what she wanted to do. No, tonight she would go to her cabin, giving Janet time to explain and Joshua space to think.

* * * *

Mitch Mathews grappled with his conflicting feelings. He had known Janet Ryden since she was a little girl. When she was twelve years old, she had gone missing and he was the young officer, fresh out of the academy and still in training, who had found her. It had been a cold, dark night, and she had been stuck up a tree, shivering and crying. He had never forgotten the protectiveness he had felt as he rescued her and cradled her cold little body against his.

For years after, she obviously had a teenage crush on him and he had gently ignored her, never being unkind but always a little distant. As she matured, she developed into a lovely young woman but, to him, she was always the little girl he'd rescued. He didn't see much of her in her later teens and then she went away to university. When he next saw her, nearly a year later, it was different. He hadn't recognized her at first because she was wearing dark sunglasses, and her hair, which she usually wore in a ponytail, was loose and flowing down her back. She had looked sophisticated and stunning, and his cock had hardened when she gave him a smoldering, sexy smile. Not being shy with the ladies, he was about to move closer when the smile changed and grew. He immediately saw who it was. She'd always had the sunniest of smiles. He had felt like a pervert, although suddenly the nine-year age gap didn't seem so bad. Since then, he'd feigned romantic indifference, expecting that she would outgrown him, but somehow each time they met there was a little bit more of an edge.

"Can I ask what's going on with Josh?" It was a safe subject.

"Oh, just a misunderstanding between him and Rachael. I need to talk to my brother to explain a few things." She briefly squeezed his arm affectionately. "Thanks for your help, I'm sorry to cut short your time at the dance."

"Don't be. I don't mind." He smiled at her. The feel of her sweet, gentle touch lingered on his skin.

They drove in silence for most of the way, but as they entered Sweet Water, she suddenly exhaled as if she had been holding her breath.

"Don't you like me, Mitch?"

Her direct approach completely caught him off guard. He stiffened, putting both hands on the steering wheel, appearing to concentrate on the road. It was a minute before he answered.

"I do," he sighed heavily. "But you're only twenty-one."

"You're hardly an old man at thirty. Anyway, what does that have to do with anything?"

"I suppose it's not such an issue now but…" He trailed off, trying to find the words.

"You know, Rachael said that it's sometimes hard for people to see when a particular pattern of behavior isn't relevant anymore; I've grown up, in case you haven't noticed."

"I've noticed, all right." Noticed and secretly coveted. He explained sadly, "It's not only that. I guess I think that you'll quickly outgrow me. I'm a deputy. Maybe I'll make sheriff one day if I work hard. You'll soon be a college graduate with a world of opportunities. I don't want to restrict you."

"So you're saying I'm too good for you?"

"No," he paused, trying to articulate exactly what he did mean, "yes. You have part ownership of a cattle and oil empire, for heaven's sake."

"Bullshit." She sounded angry now. "How dare you think that I'm the type of woman who bothers about that? If anyone is bothered, it's you!"

"Janet, it's not like that. How long would you be satisfied with the type of lifestyle I could give you?"

Janet sat back, looking shocked and very angry, "Oh, I'm seeing a different side to you now, you arrogant ass. You're too proud to consider that it wouldn't be my lifestyle changing but yours. I wouldn't mind so much if it was because you thought that you couldn't make me happy, couldn't love me or keep me satisfied. At least that would be a reason really about us and not about you and your pride!"

"Now wait a minute. You're twisting my words." He swerved to a stop in the yard near her house. "I think that you've had a schoolgirl crush on me for a long time, but maybe it's based on some unrealistic idea of who you think I am."

"No, you listen. Be honest with yourself and me. Yes, I've had a thing for you for years, Mitch Mathews. I know you're a deputy, and I love your commitment to your job. I've never considered it an obstacle to a relationship with you. I love the fact that you're strong yet gentle, hard but kind. You're a good man with a hint of bad boy in you, and I like it. Don't you see anything about me that you like, or is it only my age, money, education, and options—which apparently don't include you—that you're concerned about?" She was getting really worked up now. "All the material stuff is irrelevant unless it's a façade to hide the fact that you haven't got any balls!"

He sat still, stunned as he replayed her words. *She's right.* He suddenly realized that Janet wasn't a girl anymore. She had grown up, knew her own mind, and apparently, she wanted him.

Janet was still filled with righteous indignation. "You're also a stupid ass for not seeing what's right in front of your nose." She grabbed the door handle.

"Stay right here," he shouted, pointing at her seat.

"Screw you," she yelled back, and before he could grab her, she fell out of the vehicle. "Goddamn." She struggled to her feet and started to run.

Using long, fast strides usually reserved for running down fleeing suspects it gave him a few crucial moments to reach her. He was upon her before she made it to the house, tackling her from behind but turning to take the fall on his back.

"What the f—"

He cut off her curse with a crushing kiss, holding her head with one hand, keeping her pressed against him with the other. When he finally released her, she was breathless. He gently rolled her over and stood up, pulling her with him.

"I'm sorry. You're right. I'm a stupid, selfish ass."

"I didn't say all of that." She was breathing hard, still recovering from his kiss.

"Well, it's true. I invented reasons why you shouldn't love me when I could have been giving you reasons why you should. I've been a fool." He kissed her again, gently this time, savoring the flavor of her lips and mouth, taking her breath in. When he spoke again, his voice was deep and gravelly "The problem was my pride and lack of confidence in you. You've been on my mind and in my heart for years. Will you give me a chance to love you in the way you deserve?"

The kiss they'd shared and her words had completely shattered his resolve to stay away from her.

"God, you're actually romantic. Who knew?"

He shrugged. "Or failing that, will you settle for lots of mind-blowing sex?" *Her brothers are gonna kill me.*

She flushed pink.

"I don't think that Josh is home yet. His car isn't here," he observed hopefully.

"He will be soon, and I need to have a good, long talk with him. I'd love to invite you in but—"

"But the time's not right. I'm going to Austin tomorrow for a firearms workshop until Tuesday. I'll call you when I get back, okay?"

"You'd better because, Deputy, you're on probation. Have a good think about what I've said, Mitch Mathews, and if you are even half

the man I hope you are, you'll spend the future making it up to me."
She started toward the door of the house but then stopped to add,
"And you'd better use some imagination."

He watched her enter the house without a backward glance. For a
few moments, he couldn't bring himself to move. He wanted to go
after her but knew she had a family matter to deal with, so he
reluctantly headed home. Soon, however, he was smiling.
Imaginative? I can do that.

* * * *

Calming down, Janet leaned heavily against the door. *You'd better
use some imagination.* She groaned inwardly at her words. *Where the
hell did that come from?* Janet wasn't exactly Ms. Sexually
Experienced. In fact, she was the opposite. What the heck had she set
herself up for? She'd overheard some of the ranch hands joke that a
night with the deputy left a girl bowlegged in the morning.
Apparently, all of his big, broad, hard body was in proportion. Well,
lucky her, she hoped.

She knew that Mitch cared, but he hadn't believed that she really
wanted him. She had not-so-secretly loved him for nine years and
he'd thought that it was some childish crush. He probably believed
that he had been doing the noble thing, standing back so that she
could get on with some fantastical high-flying lifestyle he'd envisaged
for her. Well, he was in no doubt how she felt now. On the journey
home she had thought about Rachael and her misunderstanding with
Joshua. She'd resolved not to make the same mistake and, for once,
had taken a more direct approach. The next move had to be his,
though, and it had better be soon because she was going back to
college in two weeks.

She heard his truck leaving and turned on the house lights.
Obviously, Joshua wasn't home and he wasn't answering his mobile,
so she sat back on the big leather sofa to wait. She turned the TV on

to keep awake, but before long she was snoozing, and by midnight she was fast asleep.

* * * *

Joshua had decided to stay away from the house for a while. He went to the place where he sought solitude and strength—where his parents were buried at the ranch, on Lookout hill. He turned the car's lights off and stood in front of the graves in the pale moonlight. It was like a balm to his soul, and he calmly thought things through. When he'd left her on the dance floor, he'd also abandoned the hope that he had finally found the right woman, one who might be able to handle him and give as much as she could take. With Rachael, he had began to think of all the wonderful possibilities that life still had in store for him. Now that had been sucked away, leaving a vacuum of disappointment.

He hardly knew Rachael, yet he felt a connection unlike any he had ever experienced. It went beyond physical attraction, although that had plenty to do with it. He admired and respected her, too. She was certainly a strong, passionate woman, and he'd thought she'd be able to take him on. He'd been anticipating the challenge and was sure that he'd detected a hint of sin about her that attracted him even more. Clearly, his own feelings had clouded his judgment. He had incorrectly assumed she felt the same way. What made it worse was that she wanted his brother. He cursed himself for the fool he was. He'd thought that their encounter had been more than good sex, but apparently she hadn't.

How the hell was this all going to work out? As he sat quietly, a realization came to him as it often did in this place. There was nothing he could do about it, nothing at all. That didn't sit well with him. He wasn't used to being passive, but for a change, he'd have to let the tide of fate ebb and flow and deal with whatever washed up as best he could.

When Joshua finally arrived home, he saw no cars in front of the house but the lights were on. He heard noise coming from the TV room and went to investigate, hoping that it wasn't James. He didn't want to talk about tonight with James. But then, if James wasn't home, who was he with? For the first time ever, he felt jealousy toward his brother. It was a horrible, gnawing thing in the pit of his stomach and he didn't care for it one bit. He found his sister curled up asleep on the sofa, so he carefully covered her with a blanket, turned down the lights, and switched off the TV. No doubt she had intended to talk to him about Rachael, but he didn't want to disturb her. It could wait until the light of a new day.

Chapter 4

Joshua found it difficult to sleep but must have dropped off at some point because he was rudely awakened at dawn by an incessant shaking that wouldn't go away.

"W–What? What's the matter? What time is it?"

"Time you sat up and listened to me."

As he slowly heaved himself up, Janet thrust a cup of fresh coffee under his nose. "You'll need this." She then proceeded to tell him about her conversation with Rachael. The further she got with the explanation, the more alert he became.

"She's staying at Flora's Place." She paused and cocked her head to one side. "So what are you waiting for?"

"Er," he hesitated, "for you to leave. I'm naked."

"Oh, right. Well, I'll just leave you to it," she muttered, hastily backing out of his room.

Joshua showered quickly, shaved, and pulled on a pair of jeans, a T-shirt, and a light jacket. He grabbed the toast that Janet offered and kissed her on the cheek as he walked out of the door. Flora's Place was only twenty minutes away as the crow flies. It was faster by horse than car, so he saddled up Star, his stallion, and headed out at a steady canter.

While he rode, he hoped that she still wanted to see him. He was delighted that she didn't want James or the ménage lifestyle and that she had confessed to liking—no—"fancying the pants off him." He knew she was uncertain because she was basically new to Meadow Ridge, and they hadn't known each other long, but he wasn't going to let her get away. Not this one. She was going to be his.

* * * *

Rachael's alarm went off at 5:45 a.m. She slapped her hand around on the bedside table a few times before eventually hitting the off button. Slowly, she emerged from underneath the duvet, questioning her own foolish enthusiasm the night before when she had set the alarm for an early morning run. Exercise cleared her mind, and she always felt energized after a good workout. It really didn't seem like such a great idea now, but she knew that once she got a strong coffee down, she would be ready to go. She fell out of bed, forgetting that the old four-poster was higher than modern bed frames. Bleary-eyed, she tugged on a pair of running shorts, a cut off exercise top, and a pair of thick sports socks before shoving her feet into her new trail-running sneakers. Now, where had she put the coffee?

As she sipped her drink, she decided that today she would go to the Sweet Water Ranch and speak to Joshua. She would feel an idiot, but she was not the type of woman to let a misunderstanding on her behalf go uncorrected, and she thought that he wasn't the type, either. She hadn't decided if starting a relationship at this time was a good idea or not. She was aware that she was assuming that he still wanted her. *What did Janet say about* assuming? First, she wanted improve her mood and work off the annoyance that she felt with herself. A good three-mile run should do it. She headed out, setting a fast pace while listening to her iPod.

* * * *

As Joshua neared the boundary of his property, he thought he saw something moving in the opposite direction. Thinking that it could be an animal of some kind, he took his binoculars out of his saddlebag for a closer look. Astonished, he saw Rachael running through the trees, heading back toward her cabin. Joshua followed her, realizing that she wasn't aware of him. The thought left him cold. Anyone could have sneaked up on her. He'd have a word with her about it later.

She picked up the pace for two hundred yards, then slowed to a brisk walk for the last one hundred. Once she reached her cabin, she started to hit and kick the hell out of a punch bag that hung on the porch.

She was covered in sweat, and the little beads of perspiration glittered like diamonds on her skin. He watched her punish the bag with surprising ferocity. No wonder her body was so toned. He could clearly see defined muscles on her legs, exposed by high-cut shorts. Her back, shoulders, and arms also looked taut, yet there were womanly curves too. Her ass looked firm and supple but not skinny: "just big enough to park your bike in," his Irish granddaddy would have said. Right now, he was thinking about parking something else between those firm buttocks. *She's magnificent.*

* * * *

When she had finished with one last hard punch and a grunt, she removed her earphones.

"Sure hope you never get pissed off at me," a voice behind her drawled.

Rachael whirled around red faced and panting with exertion. She couldn't believe it. There was Joshua Ryden on his horse about ten yards away. *Damn, I didn't hear him. How long has he been there?* She made a mental note to herself not to play her music so loud in the future. He stared at her intently for a few seconds and then, gracefully like a big cat, swung down from the saddle. She couldn't help but notice his long legs and muscular thighs—thighs meant for riding horses...and women. Thighs that would look good between her legs. *God, what am I thinking?* As he turned around for a moment to tie the bridle to her porch, she took in his gorgeous denim-clad ass. She almost groaned but swallowed hard instead, managing to pull herself together in time. She took an involuntary step back as he prowled toward her.

"You startled me. I didn't realize anyone was here," she said with her hand going to her heart as she recovered her breath. She felt her face flush redder and was thankful that she had an excuse.

"Well, you wouldn't with those things stuck in your ears."

"Point taken." She conceded, fidgeting on the spot.

As his fierce gaze dragged down her body, she became aware that she was hot and very sweaty. Beads of perspiration slowly rolled down her neck and chest and disappeared down the cleavage of her high breasts. Her clothes clung to her and her shorts showed damp patches at the top of her thighs. She must look and smell like a dog's dinner but, strangely, one that he looked like he wanted to eat.

He took a step closer, and his nostrils flared. She heard a low deep rumbling sound, and it made her yearn for his intimate touch again.

"Just, you know, keeping fit, venting some frustration." She gave a quick nervous smile.

He blinked slowly and in a deep, low voice drawled, "Yeah, I've heard that intense physical activity is supposed to be good for stress." He smiled wickedly. "Although I can think of other, more fun and engaging ways."

He surprised her with that line. She didn't think that teasing came naturally to him.

Rachael's heart raced faster, and before she could stop herself, she was squeaking her automatic response. "Yes, well, can I help you with anything?"

She realized how it stupid and uptight it sounded as soon as the words were out, but before she could babble on further, he growled, "Yes, most definitely."

He cleared the distance between them in a heartbeat and leaned down to cover her lips with his. *We need to talk. I need a shower. But, oh, it's so good.* Her thoughts swirled just before her brain shut down and instinct took over. She parted her lips under the pressure of his passionate kiss, and she was swept away by the sensations flooding her, causing her to melt against him. She moaned as one hand caught up in her hair and the other brushed down her spine, rested on her ass, and pulled her in even closer. Unconsciously, she shifted and slipped a leg either side of his, squeezed herself around it, and rubbed slightly against him. He gave a throaty growl in response and deepened the kiss. She was lost to it, couldn't think straight, and wanted more. Her juices flowed and her core muscles clenched with anticipation. Her hands mirrored his, one reaching up around his shoulder and the other firmly cupping his backside before slipping around his hip and tentatively rubbing up the length of his barely contained erection.

He groaned again and the vibration transferred from his mouth to hers, conveying his passion. Her whole body hummed with desire. His hand roamed from her ass to her chest and pulled down the front of her sports top to expose her breasts. Gently, he stroked the back of his hand over a very sensitive erect nipple before palming and squeezing the whole globe of satin-soft flesh. It was her turn to moan as his mouth left hers and trailed kisses down her neck before stopping between her boobs and taking a long lick. *Oh, God.* It was erotic and animalistic and her pelvic floor fluttered.

He locked his mouth over a breast and sucked, flicking the nipple with his tongue before doing the same to the other. More fluttering; hell, her pussy must have developed muscle memory. She stroked her fingers through his thick hair and arched toward him. Oh, Lord, she felt consumed. She felt vibrations deep inside, she felt—wait, she *did* feel vibrations, persistent vibrations—bloody hell, her cell phone was ringing!

His passion-roughened voice sounded next to her ear as he moved up her neck to kiss her there. "Christ, ignore it."

She wanted to, *really* wanted to. She wasn't on call, but who would be ringing before seven in the morning? It could be an emergency. With one hand still in his hair, she righted her top.

"I can't," she sighed, looking at her phone and seeing Colin's name flash up.

She pulled his hair so that his forehead rested briefly against hers, then pushed against his firm chest, stepped back, took a deep breath, and answered her mobile.

"Hello, Colin, is everything all right?"

She was suddenly all business, and began to pace back and forth along the veranda, concentrating fiercely on the phone conversation. She looked at him and covered the phone with her hand. "Do you know where the Jackson Water Hole is?"

"Yeah," he sighed miserably. "It's about four miles from here as the crow flies, but about twenty if you take the road."

"Can I take my Jeep there, off road?"

"Not across the Sweet River. That's what your stream eventually flows into. The crossing place is only suitable for a horse."

"How long would it take for you to ride there with two?"

"About twenty-five minutes, much faster than you'd get there by car."

His answer was firm and precise. She nodded then turned, rapidly speaking into the phone before closing the call.

Feeling frustrated but resigned, she explained. "That was Colin. Roy Crossling's had an accident at the water hole. He's okay, but he thinks his horse was bitten on the face by a snake, a cottonmouth. Colin knows I'm staying here and was wondering if I could get there quickly and help until he arrives with the horse box and antivenom kit. If you can take me there, I can at least ease the animal's suffering. I have an emergency kit in the house." She looked at him expectantly.

"What? You're going to help that bastard Crossling?"

"No, I'm going to help that bastard Crossling's horse."

She dashed into the house. There was no time to take a shower. She threw on a pair of baggy khaki trousers, and grabbed a small pack with her white coat and the emergency kit inside. She then found a long knife and cut two pieces off the garden hose. If necessary, it could be used to keep the horse's nostrils open and thereby prevent suffocation as its tissues swelled in response to the venom.

"Life around you is certainly never boring," he commented as she jumped down the cabin's steps to where he was waiting on Star. "Here," he held out his arm, "grab a hold and swing up behind me."

"Okay, Tonto."

"*You're* Tonto. *I'm* the Lone Ranger—it's my horse."

"Whatever you say, ke-mo sah-bee. Let's go." She deftly swung up and settled herself behind him.

"Hold on tight."

"Oh, I intend to."

After about fifteen minutes of cantering, they came to the river where they slowed down to cross.

"Oh, bugger it," she groaned. "You know what that horrid Crossling is going to think when I turn up with you at this time in the morning."

"If Colin had phoned an hour later, he'd be right," he growled.

She couldn't think of what to say. To deny it would make her a liar. What was she doing? This was so unlike her. She had her professional reputation to think of and had worked too hard, in what was mainly a man's world, to fall foul of disparaging gossip now, yet she couldn't bring herself to regret her reaction to Joshua. He rang all her bells and then some. Just sitting so snug against him as his butt ground against her mound was driving her crazy with every sway from the horse's gait. She was jolted from her musings when they started to canter again, and sure enough, about ten minutes later, the water hole came in sight.

Roy Crossling looked surprised to see the lady vet and Ryden. Both had belittled him, and he hated them for it. Together so early in the morning could only lead to one conclusion in his mind.

"Well, well," he smirked, "sorry to interrupt you."

Both Joshua and Rachael ignored him. It was the horse they were here to see, and it was laboring hard to breathe.

"I'm going to open his airways with the hose pipe and then inject an anti-inflammatory to slow the swelling and antibiotic to prevent infection. That should help until Colin gets here with the antivenin." Rachael quickly set about her tasks.

"That's a lot of 'antis.' Are you qualified?" he sneered.

"Yes, Crossling, I am, but I am not yet licensed to practice here. If you have a problem with that, please say so now and your horse can die."

Roy stayed silent as she worked, keeping as much distance as practical between himself and Joshua. Rachael was soothing the horse as best as she could when Colin finally arrived. She was relieved. The sooner the antivenin was injected, the better the chance that the horse would survive. Colin set to work, then loaded the animal into the horse box.

"Another good effort, Rach, thanks. Thanks to you, too, Josh. I'll take the horse back with me." He looked from Rachael to Joshua and gave her an amused, knowing look "You don't need to come. All the work's been done. It's just a case of keeping him under observation."

"Okay, let me know how he's doing later."

"When are you thinking of starting work?" Colin queried.

"Well, I was hoping to take another week off to do some local exploring and put the final finishing touches to the cabin. Of course, if you need any help in that time, just call."

"That's a great idea, and thanks for the help again."

Crossling said nothing to Rachael and went with Colin without a backward glance. She noted that he avoided Joshua's hostile glare and gave him a wide berth. Standing next to Joshua, she could feel the dominant aura that radiated from him. It reminded her of an alpha male dog, or more like a wolf. They rarely had to fight because their sheer size and assured presence was enough. In a pack, they were never the jumpy, yappy animals, but the calmer, more aloof ones. Until now, she hadn't met a human male who was so obviously an alpha, and it really turned her on. It was most disconcerting. She felt like a bitch in heat.

Rachael moved away from Joshua to try to clear her mind. She collected her gear together and stowed her white coat in the backpack.

"You know Crossling is not going to keep his mouth shut." She sighed. "He's a slimy individual."

"Do you care?" He was watching her intently.

"No, not really. After all, there have always been rumours about the Lone Ranger and Tonto." She tried to smile. "Seriously, though, I do care about my reputation, professional and personal. I'm definitely not a prude, but I don't do casual, Josh, despite what happened." She couldn't withhold a blush.

"I know."

"I made an incorrect assumption last night, and I'm sorry, but it just shows that we don't know each other very well."

"Yet," he said firmly. "But I like what I've seen so far." He moved closer, leaned down, slowly picked her up, and held her close in a soft embrace before placing her on his horse. "Come on, I'll take you back to the cabin." He swung up behind her and shifted close. With his legs firmly planted either side of hers, they cantered back toward her cabin.

Rachael's heart was racing. Being this close to the man made breathing difficult. That he sat tight up against and behind her amplified the reaction. She felt both protected and vulnerable, which sent a shiver down her spine. From this position, he was in control, and she relished it. He was so big, virile, and masculine, but not intimidating—not to her, anyway—although she knew he had that affect on others. He made her feel feminine and as sexy as hell. Joshua Ryden was by far the most interesting individual she had ever met. He was clearly a capable man, used to being the boss, and that appealed to her on some primal level. She decided to take the bull by the horns and ask the question that intrigued her most.

"Joshua, why don't you want the same lifestyle as your parents? They were happy, weren't they?"

"Very."

"So?"

He spoke slowly but fluidly, which suggested that he had given a lot of thought to the issue. "For a number of reasons. First, although I have friends, there isn't another man I'm that close to. The only person I'd consider is James. I'll be honest with you, we have experimented casually."

Kinky and erotic images formed in Rachael's mind, and she couldn't help squirming between his thighs, unavoidably grinding back against his groin.

As he continued, he sounded strained. "Although James is his own man, I don't think that it would be healthy for him to always be in the role of younger brother. A ménage relationship with me would only reinforce that role. Second, James and I have different," he paused to find the right words, "desires. Sexual needs." When he spoke, his voice was low and his lips were close to her ear. "I'm a dominant man, Rachael, especially in bed."

In response, she felt a shiver course down her spine and a flush of moisture between her legs, and she shifted in the saddle. He could not be unaware of her reaction, and she felt her face redden. His thighs pressed more firmly against her—yes, he knew.

"James likes to share. I don't. I want you all to myself. I want you to be mine, nobody else's."

She squirmed again. He was so intense. "And what about you? I'd demand the same."

He snorted. "I don't take demands, darlin'. I make them." He paused as she stiffened. "But, from you, I'd expected no less."

When they arrived at the cabin, he dismounted first, then helped her. He slid her slowly down his hard body and stopped her when her eyes were level with his and her feet were still dangling off the ground. His face was so close that their noses almost touched.

"You really do smell good enough to eat." He growled as he buried his face in the nape of her neck and kissed a sweet spot that sent tremors across her shoulders and down her spine again.

She swooned slightly for a moment, feeling almost drunk on desire for him. *Oh, God, I want to shag your socks off.*

"Er, very soon I'm going to smell good enough to bury. I really need to take a shower."

"Do you want me to go?" he asked reluctantly, as if it were the last thing that he wanted to do.

"No." She startled herself with the certainty of her response. "Why don't you see to Star while I take a shower, and then we'll talk?"

"If I come in, we'll do more than talk."

She froze at his words and the hunger in his eyes. He regarded her like a predator staring down its prey. She was mesmerized for a few seconds. Then, consumed by a desire too strong to deny, she attacked first and kissed him savagely, wrapping her legs around his waist, invading his mouth with her tongue. He responded briefly then pulled back, breathing raggedly.

"You'd better go and get that shower right now, or we won't make it through the door."

As he lowered her to the ground, she slid along the length of his erection, which caused him to groan. Her pussy clenched, the inner walls longing to grasp his cock tightly, turning slick in anticipation.

"I'm getting stiff. I didn't stretch after my run, and I need a long hot shower to relax my muscles."

"I'm already stiff, and if you haven't finished before I've seen to Star, you can bet it *will* be a long, hot shower." He gave her a slow, wicked smile.

Jesus, he aroused her like no other, enflaming her desire. It was implausible, yet he was so compelling. In a flustered state, she backed away, made it shakily to her bedroom, and had to peel off her wet panties. Once naked, she scrutinized herself in the mirror. Thankfully, she had shaved and plucked the day before in preparation for the dance. She could see the glistening wetness of her full pussy lips and couldn't help conjuring the erotic imagine of Joshua's cock nestled between the folds.

Once in the shower, Rachael let the hot water stream over her head and down her body to relieve the tension in her muscles. The room quickly filled with steam. As she shampooed her hair, she heard the click of the shower door opening and closing behind her. He must have dealt with his horse in double-quick time, and the thought pleased her greatly.

Keeping her back to him, she continued to wash until big hands clasped her wrists and gently pulled her arms forward to rest her palms on the tiled wall in front. She stood in that position, leaning against the wall without saying a word as the water beat down on her shoulders. His hands then continued the job, massaging her scalp slowly and firmly. It felt wonderful. He pulled her head back to rinse the suds away and leaned down to kiss her neck, quickly finding the sweet spot halfway down that sent a shiver through her body. He lathered his hands with the unperfumed soap. Rachael could faintly detect the pleasant, heady, combined fragrance of their bodies in the steamy air.

She felt his hands reverently move across her shoulders and down her body, stroking her lightly, not missing a spot, not stopping once. He crouched and lifted one foot and then the other, taking the time to massage her toes and soles. His hands ran firmly up her legs and over her butt and swept around her hips to her thighs. When he reached her pussy, he stopped for a second as he registered that it was bare. She heard his sharp intake of breath, felt the long exhale on the small of her back. With excruciating slowness, he slid his hand between her legs and a thick finger into her slick opening. Her wetness had nothing to do with the water and soap and everything to do with him. She moaned, but stayed in the position that he had placed her. He rose up again behind her, keeping his hand between her legs while his other arm wrapped her in an embrace that brought her into contact with him. He was all hard muscle and warm skin, and she itched to touch him.

Sensing that she was about to move he kissed her neck again and whispered in her ear, "Don't move, sweetheart."

"But I want to see you and touch you."

"I know. Soon."

He rolled a nipple between his fingers and she gasped. He softly kneaded first one breast then the other before gliding away back down to her pussy. He deftly transferred hands, placing another thick finger inside her and his thumb on her clit. The one he'd removed was coated in her cream and he brought it to the entrance of her ass. He swirled his finger around the puckered skin before slowly easing it inside. He paused for a moment, as if gauging her response to the more risqué intimate invasion. She didn't protest because it felt good—naughty, but oh-so-nice. He moved his fingers, synchronizing the motion to heighten her pleasure while kissing and nipping her nape.

It was incredibly arousing and she began to pant and moan with pleasure.

"Oh, God, Josh, I'm going to come if you keep this up."

"That's the idea."

"What about you?"

He voice was deep and darkly seductive. "We have plenty of time and you can have multiple orgasms, so come for me, beautiful…now."

At exactly that moment, she felt the tremors start. She writhed on his hands as her pussy and ass clenched on his fingers. A cry of abandonment left her mouth as she gave herself up to the sensations. Her hips bucked, and her cunt went into a spasm. Her legs buckled and trembled as she slid down to her knees. Joshua went with her, keeping his hands in place, providing some support.

Breathing rapidly, Rachael stayed still for a minute, on her knees with her hands resting on the wall. Slowly, he slid his fingers from her, which caused a gasp to escape her lips.

"You are incredibly sexy," he murmured as he nuzzled her neck.

"You bring it out," she panted.

He stood, grabbed a washcloth, lifted her to her feet, and switched off the shower. She was about to turn around to see him properly, but he swept her up in his arms.

"Where's your bedroom?"

She pointed the way, amazed that he carried her as if she weighed nothing at all. As they left the bathroom she snaffled a big, plush bath towel that was hanging by the door.

"Nice bed," he commented as they entered her room. "Good sturdy posts."

He deposited her on the end then took a step back. She was able to see him in all his glory, and he was glorious, no doubt about it. He was over six and a half feet of work-hardened muscle. There was a small patch of hair in the middle of his chest and groin, but otherwise his tanned skin was smooth. His large, erect cock jutted up from a set of very impressively sized balls.

"I see that you have something in common with your bull," she wryly observed.

"Yep, and we both like you, darlin'." He smirked, and then abruptly his smile fell. "Drop the towel and open your legs, Harrison."

"W–What?"

He said nothing else. His mouth was set in a hard line, no hint of a smile, and he continued to stare at her intently, waiting. Unbelievably, her thighs parted as if of their own volition.

"Wider. I want to see your dripping cunt."

Her mouth watered at his crude words and she gulped. She found his dominance exhilarating. Not taking her eyes off his face, she splayed her legs even further open. He could now clearly see the engorged, cream-coated lips of her bare pussy.

"You were right about not being a prude. Dirty talk turns you on, doesn't it, Rachael?" He continued to stare between her legs.

"Yes," she croaked, closing her eyes, feeling vulnerable and mortified to find that he knew her so well.

"Open your eyes," he commanded. "I have to have a taste, and I want you to watch."

Yep, there was muscle memory stored in her pussy, all right, because it was sure getting excited.

He stepped toward her then reached passed to grab some pillows to prop her up on. He pushed her back gently and knelt between her legs, levering them even wider open with his broad shoulders.

"So beautiful," he murmured and blew softly on her clit.

It was an intensely erotic act for her to watch as Joshua snaked his tongue around her swollen flesh and then lapped along her slit before plunging deeper. An internal pressure began to build between her legs and in the pit of her stomach.

"Mmm, delicious."

He kept eye contact for several seconds before closing his own with a look of ecstasy on his face as he slowly and skilfully devoured her. For several minutes, Rachael was lost to his unequalled oral ministrations.

"You taste so good. I could do this all day," he groaned.

"But I want more." She was breathing faster now, restless and roused, needing to be filled and stretched.

"Darlin', why am I not surprised?"

"You know why."

Kindred spirit came to mind.

"Tell me, Rachael, tell me what you want."

She held his fierce, lust-ridden gaze and sensed a tipping point. Should she be brazen or demure? What did he expect of the lady vet?

This was not a time for deception, and she opted for honesty. She spoke slowly, in clear, precise English tones.

"I want your big, wide, hard cock shoved so far up my cunt that I feel your balls slap my ass as you fuck me hard."

* * * *

Joshua nearly choked. He had not expected such a graphic, lewd answer and almost came right there and then. Jesus, this was the woman he'd been waiting for. Most people were intimidated by him, not her. She was an enigma—sometimes cool, sometimes hot, reserved or wanton, focused then lost to passion, submissive and now demanding.

"Well, if that's what you want—"

"But," she interrupted, "first I want to taste you. I want to lick and suck your impressive cock and balls." She looked at him with an impish smile on her lips and gleam in her eye.

"Hell, woman, if you keep talking like that I won't last five minutes."

"I'll shut up then." She smiled slyly. "Or maybe you could find something to gag me with?"

For the first time ever, he was being led. By God, she was a challenge, and it turned him on intensely. He grabbed a handful of her damp hair and kissed her hard and deep. When he broke off the kiss, her face looked flushed with desire.

"Get on all fours," he said, taking charge again, and she obeyed, facing him at the end of the bed. "Suck me," he demanded, holding his cock near her mouth, keeping a hand in her hair.

She complied by lightly licking the large, glistening, bulbous head before swiping her tongue around its girth. He gasped. With one hand, she cupped his balls and massaged gently as she licked her way down his length to the base. There she nipped and sucked at his sac, which caused him to groan even louder, before running her tongue to the sensitive place between his balls and anus. His hips swayed slightly, and he widened his stance. He took a sharp shallow breath as she briefly played around the entrance to his ass with a wet finger, teasing the puckered skin but going no further.

Nobody had touched him there before, and it felt amazing. She then licked her way back to the base of his cock and up around the tip, where she rested for a moment to catch his eyes with hers. Slowly, holding his gaze, she parted her lips and sank her hot, wet mouth down, closing her eyes with a look of bliss as she did so. A little moan rose from her throat. Keeping her lips tightly clamped around him, she took him to the back of her throat before placing a hand around the rest of his erection at the base. Good, he was big and he didn't want her to choke or gag. She slid up and down his length with her mouth and hand, maintaining a steady rhythm and pressure, swirling her tongue around the end and tickling under the rim of the head. His hips began to pump back and forth, and his grip in her hair tightened.

"Jesus H. Christ," he rasped. "That feels so good." She really was an excellent cock sucker and he knew that if he didn't pull away he'd shoot his load down her throat. Appealing though that thought was, he wanted to fuck her pussy; taking control again he pulled her away gently by her hair. "Face the other way."

She looked wanton and yet submissively sensual as she did as she was told. Holding her by the hips he pulled her back toward the edge of the bed, knees spread wide.

"Do you have any condoms nearby?" He had some in the pocket of his jeans but they had been discarded in haste, somewhere in the living room. He didn't want to leave her to go hunting for them.

"No, they're in the bathroom, but I'm not sure that they'd fit you anyway." She looked over her shoulder at him as he stood close behind her. "I appreciate the gesture but you don't need to bother on my account. After all, it's a bit like shutting the stable door after the horse has bolted."

He stilled. There was nothing he'd like more than to skin dive into her warm, wet channel.

"You're the only women I haven't worn one with," he confessed. *The only, the first, and maybe the last.*

He dipped his thumb into her slit and coated it with her slick cream. Then he slid it back to her tightly puckered rosette. Clutching his dick in his other hand, he placed it at her engorged, red entrance and rubbed the tip back and forth along the glistening seam. He slowly pushed forward, tunnelling between the soft, warm flesh and groaned at the sensation of her strong muscles yielding snugly around his shaft. Riding her bareback was an incomparable, sublime experience. As he forged forward with his cock, he pressed his thumb through the tight ring of her ass. They both moaned in unison, and he felt the involuntary clenching of her muscles.

"Lord, Rachael, I feel your heat and your pussy gripping me. Fucking beautiful."

Holding still, giving her muscles time to adjust, he turned his attention to her ass, slowly moving his thick thumb in and out. Then with shallow strokes he began to pump into her.

"Sweetheart, you were built for sin."

She pushed back against him. He took that as a cue to lengthen his strokes but maintained a slow pace, which allowed her to undulate her hips. She tried to reach back to clasp his balls but he stopped her hand.

"Uh-uh, I don't need any more stimulation than you're giving me, darlin'. I want this to last." He wasn't about to blow his load like a young buck desperate for a fuck. Who was he trying to kid? Fact of the matter was that he *was* desperate, and it took all of his self-discipline not to ravish her.

He pushed his thumb as far as it would go into her and worked it back and forth in time with the slow pumping of his cock. Then he stopped and wound an arm around her waist to guide her to an upright position. Her muscles tightened around his hand and cock, adjusting to the new angle of penetration.

"Put one arm around my neck."

She reached up and back to comply. He kissed her nape and ran his free hand over her breasts, stomach and mound before alighting on her clit, which he caressed with a light circular motion. He wanted her to come one more time before they found release together. She began to tremble as he increased the pressure of his finger.

"Oh God, oh God, Joshua," she screamed as she ground down on his thumb and cock, drawing him deeper with strong silky muscles clasping his length. He stilled, waited until the initial ripples subsided, then slowly bent her forward again, only farther than before, so that she was resting low on her shoulders with her ass high. It was a totally submissive position, leaving him highly aroused.

He removed his thumb slowly, and she gasped as her muscles closed behind it. Wiping himself on the washcloth, he then ran his hands over her ass. The sight of her presented this way excited him more than he could have imagined. He was filled with carnal lust.

Grabbing hold of her hips, he withdrew almost completely from her pussy and then plunged forward, impaling her hard and deep. He felt his cockhead butt the end of her cervix.

"Oh, you're so big," she cried, moving back to grind herself on him. He began to forcibly thrust into her, picking up the pace, ramming her with his cock. Their grunts and groans and the sound of his balls slapping her ass filled the room.

"Is—this—the—fucking—you—wanted?" he ground out with each powerful stroke.

He barely heard her reply through the pounding of blood in his ears, her panting, and her cries of pleasure. She pushed back, meeting his thrusts, urging him on.

"Answer me," he commanded.

"Yes—fuck—yes, it's more," she cried.

"You are mine. Say it."

"Yes."

"Say it."

"Yes, yours. I'm yours," she howled, shuddering with orgasmic spasms of release.

"Rachael!" His guttural reciprocating roar drowned out all other noise as he shot copious amounts of cum into her womb. He clasped her to him as her cunt massaged his cock with powerful contractions, the likes of which he had never before experienced. It took him over the edge to oblivion and his world wheeled around. As he pulsed, he felt as if he had died and gone to heaven—his piece of heaven, Rachael.

Unable to stand, he collapsed onto the bed, his sweat-covered body over hers, remembering just in time to take the weight on his arms and not her back. Still deep inside, he held her closer and they remained that way for several minutes, slowly regaining their breath, clearing their lust-fogged minds, coming down to earth.

Eventually, he shifted and rolled onto his side, taking Rachael with him. He kissed her shoulder and neck, drowsily playing with her nearly dry curls while she stroked his leg that was over her hip and entwined her fingers with his. She snoozed for a little while and he enjoyed the simple pleasure of holding her close.

Rachael's stomach rumbled.

"Someone's hungry."

His voice brought her back to full consciousness. Neither of them had eaten much earlier that morning, and it was now passed midday.

"Man cannot live on sex alone," she misquoted with a satisfied sigh.

"Unfortunately. Do you have any food in?"

"A little. Enough for a snack, I need to stock up."

"Okay, you prepare the food. I'll make the coffee, and we'll have that talk you mentioned earlier."

"Sounds like a plan, but I'll just take another quick shower."

He raised his eyebrow.

"Alone, or we'll never get fed." She scowled playfully.

"Okay, I'll get in when you've finished."

He slipped out of her and planted a kiss on her cheek before moving to the bathroom and wrapping a towel around his waist. Rachael couldn't keep her eyes off him, he noticed with satisfaction. She climbed off the bed and brushed past him as she headed to the shower. He grabbed her wrist and openly appraised her naked body.

"You are a beautiful woman, Miss Harrison."

He felt his libido stir again, even after such a thorough sating.

"Why, thank you, Mr. Ryden, sir," she said in her best imitation of a Southern Bell and turned toward the cubicle. She chuckled, then yelped, as he swatted her ass.

* * * *

Rachael marvelled at how familiar and comfortable it felt to have him there with her. They sat at her small dining table eating hastily assembled bacon, lettuce, and tomato sandwiches. She wore a bathrobe, and he had a towel wrapped around his waist. He had asked her lots of questions about her life in England, her family, her work, and about what she liked to do in her spare time. She found that she enjoyed telling him, relating funny stories and describing her friends.

She realized that behind the slow Texan drawl was a quick mind keeping pace with her thoughts and that he was able to discuss a wide range of topics. He was a good listener and seemed genuinely interested in her.

She didn't pry too much into his life, but he seemed to open up and talk freely with her about himself. She was pleasantly surprised at how easily he smiled and laughed with her. It was a side she suspected others didn't see much. It was hard to reconcile the relaxed man at her table with the stern, granite-faced cattle rancher.

She decided that it couldn't just be infatuation, but even though she was relaxed in his company, she was always aware of the potent sexual attraction between them simmering now just below the surface.

Rachael got up to put their plates and cups by the sink.

"Come home with me. I'll cook dinner tonight."

"You cook?" She was surprised.

"Hey, multitalented," he teased, indicating to himself. "Even I have a creative side."

"I sure bet that you do." She purred, looking him down and up.

The atmosphere changed suddenly, and sexual tension charged the air. Moving faster than seemed plausible for such a big man, he snatched her away from the sink. Reacting quickly, she pivoted and almost twisted away but couldn't break completely free as he pushed her toward the wall. Grabbing her bathrobe, he tugged it down past her shoulders, baring her breasts. She struggled, but it only served to reveal more of her body and caused his towel to fall to the floor. The sight of his stiff, ready cock and the feral, predatory gleam in his eyes thrilled, worried and excited her.

"I can't get enough of you," Joshua ground out in a lust laden voice. He kissed her roughly and pushed her hard against the wall.

Escape was unwanted and futile, but she couldn't make it too easy, either. The warped need to know what he was capable of was too strong. Intending to deny him access, she slapped her thighs together and tried to push him back with her hands on his chest. She could have been pushing against a huge boulder for all the difference it made. He easily kicked her legs apart and, keeping them pinned against his own, pushed her up the wall while gripping her buttocks and pressing his strong body against hers. With her poised over his straining cock, he stilled. He could easily impale her, and she could do nothing about it. But he waited, needing her capitulation. After several heart-thumping seconds, she acquiesced, wrapping her legs around his waist. He slammed her down, skewering her on his thick, rock-solid length. She cried out at the exquisite initial invasion and then sobbed with pleasure as he shafted her rough and hard. It was over quickly when they shouted their simultaneous climax.

After a minute, Joshua shakily carried her to the sofa and sat down, staying inside her still-quivering cunt, gently stroking her back and kissing her face.

"You're insatiable," she murmured through his kisses.

"You bring it out," he echoed back her words from the shower.

When the aftershocks subsided and her mind cleared, she realized that sex with him was the most thrilling and satisfying she had ever had. Again, he had taken her, and she had submitted. Would he be game for a bit of role reversal? An idea came to her—a way that she could explore the possibilities.

"I'll make a deal with you, Ryden. We'll play a game of chance and skill. Loser has to do whatever the winner wants for the rest of the day until midnight."

He gave her a calculating look. "Whatever the winner wants? What are the rules?" Obviously he wasn't stupid.

"Best of three games of, uh, say, poker, although it has been ages since I last played." She tried to sound nonchalant. It was her best game. "The winner has complete control. Obviously there are limits. For example, I promise not to paint your toes pink and I won't hurt you...much," she taunted. She expected to have him begging for release before the end of the night. Joshua Ryden needed to drop the reins of control occasionally, too, and she'd make sure that he enjoyed it. "You can choose the game." She smiled innocently.

A slow, sinful grin spread across his face. "Oh, poker is fine with me, although I'm a bit rusty."

"Okay, let's get dressed and then play." She eased herself off him and almost skipped to her bedroom in delight that he had so readily agreed.

He was picking up his clothes from all over the floor and dressing quickly when she returned.

"I want to avoid any misunderstanding arising from this little game we're playing, darlin'. We need a safe word. How about *red*? That word immediately calls a halt to whatever we're doing, agreed?"

Rachael paused for a moment, realising the full extent of what she'd started. Joshua certainly seemed more experienced than her, although she suspected he'd never been on the receiving end. Nevertheless, she was fairly confident that, this time, she'd be giving it to him.

"Good idea. Make sure that if necessary you say it loud and clear." She smirked.

He snorted but said nothing.

"The rules are that you can fold a maximum of three times and not lose, okay?"

"Fine with me."

Rachael slowly and clumsily dealt the cards and saw a brief expression of sympathy on Joshua's face. No doubt he was thinking that it would be like taking candy from a baby. It obviously came as somewhat of a shock to him when he lost the first hand. He sat back, slightly stunned. He'd been complacent, just as she'd planned. He should have folded but she had bluffed. She had pouted and looked unhappy with her cards, when in fact they had been good. She tried hard not to gloat.

"Wow, just lucky, I guess." She smiled sweetly at him while picking up the cards and shuffling them like a croupier. She winked at him as she expertly dealt the cards. Yep, he'd been duped and he now knew it.

"Best of three, darlin'." He reminded her.

He smiled like a politician, and she didn't trust it. Joshua won the next hand.

"Just luck, I guess." He grinned, but it had been a close thing and he didn't look quite so cocky.

The seeds of worry began to germinate in Rachael's mind. She'd bloody well miscalculated. Joshua was not a man to underestimate.

He deliberately dealt the next hand awkwardly and slowly, watching her with a sarcastic expression the entire time. The fun gleam in his eye when she had suggested the game now seemed a lot more sinister.

Stay focused on the game, Rachael.

He put his hands behind his head, looking relaxed and displaying his bulging biceps. Bastard. She knew what he was doing: trying to distract her. Keeping her eyes on her cards, she slowly licked her lips and then traced her finger around her mouth, tapped her teeth, and occasionally sneaked her tongue out to touch the finger, looking like she was concentrating hard and not being suggestive at all. When she peeked up through her eyelashes, it took all of her effort not to smirk because he was staring fiercely at her mouth.

He cleared his throat and looked at his cards. His face was a mask of neutrality.

Aha, Lady Luck loves me. Rachael was relieved to see that her hand was very strong. Ryden was in for one big shock. The guy wasn't used to losing.

Carefully schooling her features, she quizzically raised her eyebrows. "Well?"

"Mmm, I think I'll stay in." His voice gave nothing away.

"Well, okay. Me, too. Let's see what you've got." She leaned back confidently.

"Ladies first," he insisted.

She didn't mind. She had a good hand. Rachael watched his face as she laid down her full house. He remained impassive, and he continued to stare at her, probably stunned, poor thing. She tried, unsuccessfully, not to grin like the cat that got the cream.

"Oh, don't worry, Joshua," she said with barely contained glee. "You'll come to see it as a win-win situation...in the end."

"Oh, no doubt about that." He suddenly looked smug as he revealed his hand, a straight flush. Rachael blinked. No, it couldn't be.

"Bugger me," she whispered.

"I intend to," he drawled.

Her eyes popped open wide. She was lost for words.

A small smile tugged at his lips. "Grab your things. I'm taking you home to Sweet Water. I want to demonstrate my," he made little quotation marks in the air, "creative side."

Bloody hell. She knew that she was in trouble now.

Rachael packed an overnight bag, including a skirt, as instructed by Joshua. She still couldn't quite believe that she had lost the game. She had to give Ryden his due, though. He was behaving like the perfect gentleman, gracious in his victory. She wasn't sure if she trusted it, like the calm before a storm. Her pussy tingled, but her backside clenched in panic. She had never been fully taken *there*, just finger play and certainly nothing as large as his cock.

She was determined to appear cool and carefree, so when she returned to the living room, she flashed him her brightest smile.

"Ready. I'm all yours."

"Yes, you are."

She remembered her screamed declaration earlier, and judging by his expression, he did, too. She cursed her Celtic ancestry as she started to blush bright red.

"Rachael," he spoke tenderly. "Never feel embarrassed with me. It's just us, darlin'. Whatever happens is just between us."

She held his gaze and her heart flip-flopped. He looked so sincere and utterly doable, and she knew that she was falling hard. He reached out and embraced her, gently raining light kisses on her eyes, nose, cheeks, and finally mouth.

"Come on, let's go home."

Home? It wasn't her home but she like the way he said it. He picked up her bag, held her hand and walked to the Jeep.

"I'd prefer it if you came with me, but I think that you'd rather take your Jeep."

He was perceptive. She wanted to have the option to leave at any time without having to rely on anyone else.

"See you soon. No stopping along the way to help an injured fly."
He looked reluctant to leave her. Maybe he thought that she was
going to bolt.

"But they look so helpless on my windshield." She chuckled.

"That's what wipers are for."

"Oh, so cruel, but don't worry, I won't skip out on you. A deal is a
deal."

Seeing Joshua in this unexpectedly caring and charming light, she
relaxed but couldn't help wondering what he had planned for the
evening. The plans she'd had for him were quite possibly along
similar lines. Improbable though it was, she felt aroused again,
excited by hinted at dark desires.

* * * *

Joshua watched her leave and had to remind himself that she was
his for the rest of the day and all night if he could help it. He was
elated that she had just handed him the golden opportunity to explore
her kinky side with fewer inhibitions because she could tell herself it
was just part of the game. As he saddled up Star, he'd decided not to
do the obvious thing straight away but instead to spend the rest day
courting her.

He had liked listening to her tales of life in England. She clearly
loved her work and was anxious to be licensed in Texas. Not only
could she look after herself, but he also knew from the way she had
behaved toward his sister that she cared about others. She was kind to
the animals in her care, but not weak. Vets often had to make difficult
decisions when it came to dealing with creatures in pain and distress.

Joshua enjoyed the way he didn't have to over-explain things to
her. She was a good listener, and he had talked more about himself to
her than he had with anyone else outside of his immediate family.
Even so, he had omitted to mention much about their other family
business. Sure she knew that the ranch was large and that they

provided Colin with a lot of business, but she didn't appear to know about their company Sweet Oil.

Experiences with some women had taught him to be wary. His wealth had attracted gold diggers interested only in material gain. Rachael, however, didn't seem too interested in material wealth. He discovered that she enjoyed simple things like outdoor pursuits, such as hiking and running, but that she also loved to curl up at home with a good piece of fiction and a glass of wine.

Janet and James would most likely be home, so he would cook a family meal. After a little wining and dining, they would retire to his wing of the house and the real fun and games would begin. He hoped that she would stay the night.

When Janet was younger, he never had women over to stay. He always went back to their place after making sure that either James or Isabella were home. When Janet left for college, he'd had his lady friends over to the house, but even so, none had ever actually slept, *really* slept, in his bed. He had always taken them back to their homes first, even though they were usually worn out by that time. He realized that he'd been a cold bastard. He couldn't imagine sending Rachael home. He instead imagined snuggling up to her and waking next to her in the morning. It was a pleasant fiction that he wanted to make a reality, and, with that thought in mind, he mounted Star and headed for home.

Chapter 5

As Joshua approached the ranch house, he felt a warm swell of satisfaction. He preferred how the house and gardens appeared from this angle of approach—secluded and private. The large pool reflected the lazy, warm light of the afternoon onto the walls of the house, giving it an ephemeral quality and evoking calmness and serenity. The overall beauty of the gardens was a product of good landscape design, careful plant selection, irrigation, and maintenance. There were pretty pathways under the shade of jasmine vines and bougainvillea leading to secluded benches with views of the surrounding countryside. His mother had started the garden because she had wanted a relaxing haven for the family, and he had merely continued with her design ideas.

He thought of Rachael, picturing her enjoying the garden but then fractured the tranquil image with thoughts of a carnal nature: Rachael bent over a bench, up against a tree, on her knees near the fountain, and sitting on the swing seat with her legs spread wide. He adjusted his plans to include a stroll in the grounds.

It was a Sunday afternoon, and the place was quiet. Most of the ranch hands would be away until the morning. Joshua dismounted and led Star around the house and to the stables. Rachael's Jeep wasn't there. He'd arrived before her, as expected. He entered the building and discovered James checking on his own horse.

"A good night?"

"More enjoyable than yours, from what Jan tells me." James grinned.

"Well, it got better, so don't feel sorry for me."

"Really?" James said, fishing.

"A gentleman doesn't tell."

"You're not usually a gentleman."

"Well, I am today. She's on her way over here, so behave."

"Scout's honor. So I guess that means there's no chance of me getting any of that fine ass?" James ducked as Joshua took a playful swipe at him.

"She doesn't fancy you, amigo."

"So I heard. Who'd have thought that a lovely lady like Miss Harrison would have such questionable taste?"

"You and Luke can get your own. You don't seem short of company."

"We're lookin'. It's such a chore," James joked.

They fed their animals and strolled to the house just as Rachael arrived.

"Hi, guys," she called out, dazzling them with her bright smile.

Joshua felt relief and desire at the sight of her. It was ridiculous, but he didn't really care. He went to help with her bag and noted with satisfaction that she didn't resist this time. He pushed the boundaries a little further by putting an arm around her shoulders and guided her into the house.

* * * *

His large hand felt warm and her skin reacted with increased sensitivity. Her body was uncannily aware of his. It was totally unchartered territory for her.

As they walked up the wooden steps to the wide veranda and main entrance, Janet appeared with a delighted grin on her face.

"Hey, it's good to see you...both."

For a second, Rachael froze. *Jeepers, this is all happening so fast.* But then a soft squeeze from Joshua chided her out of it. So what if it was happening quickly? Not everything had a specific time frame.

"Thanks," Rachael said with a soft smile, alluding not only to the welcome but also to Janet's help in smoothing out the misunderstanding of the night before. They all took their dusty boots off before entering the house.

"Anyone fancy a nice cool beer?" Janet headed toward the gigantic fridge to a chorus of "Sure."

Joshua excused them and, with a jerk of his head, indicated that Rachael should follow. He headed toward a door at the far end of the large living room. She started to turn and caught James smirking at her as he noticed the overnight bag.

"Shut up."

James raised his eyebrows in mock shock. "Me? What?"

"*Before* you say anything." She gave him a wry grin and headed after Joshua, who had reached a solid-looking wooden door.

"The south wing of the house is where my rooms are, Janet takes the upstairs over the middle section of the house, and James takes the north side. It gives us privacy...the walls are thick," he added poignantly.

They passed through what Rachael considered a portal to Joshua's inner sanctum. She was intrigued by what lay beyond. They walked into a sizable study with dark brown leather easy chairs and an impressive, wooden, antique-looking boardroom table. In one corner was an office desk with computer and other such equipment. Books lined one wall, along with a large plasma screen. It was elegant yet practical, and Rachael immediately felt comfortable. She liked the smell of leather, polish, and man, and she couldn't help taking an audible sniff.

"Smells lovely," she explained when she noticed him watching her closely.

He smiled and led the way through another door.

"This is my bedroom, obviously."

A massive, dark wooden platform bed dominated the plain but stylish room. The headboard was a beautiful lattice work of wood.

The décor was brown and white, leather and linen. A spacious walk-in wardrobe and bathroom existed through two other doors. However, what Rachael noticed first was the large folding glass doors along the west gable end.

"Wow, you must get a spectacular view of the sunset in here. This room must turn orange. I bet it's beautiful."

"It is. I'll show you later." He gave a soft chuckle.

"What?"

"Nothing. It's just that most people notice things like the huge bed or the wall mirror. Straight away you pinned the real reason I love this room. A few years ago I had the house redesigned so that all of the bedrooms and the back veranda have a view of the sunset."

She ignored the fact that "most people" probably alluded to other women. Hell, it was to be expected. Damn. Now that he'd mentioned the bed, she did think that it was impressive and that mirror looked strategically placed. *Oh, for heaven's sake. Of course, he's had a sex life before me.* She should just consider herself lucky that she was benefiting from his experience because he sure knew his way around the female form. Still, she began to wonder just how much action that mirror had reflected. *Stop it, stop it right now!*

"It's all very lovely. You live well," she said pleasantly.

"I do, but it could be better. Come here."

"No. You come here." She lifted her chin defiantly.

He smiled like a hunter who had his prey in easy sight and took a step forward. She took a corresponding step back. They repeated the maneuver and her shins hit the end of the bed causing her to stumble onto her back. Quickly, he moved over her and planted his hands firmly either side of her shoulders, forming a human cage.

"Well, now, you're not being very obedient, sweetheart. Have you forgotten our deal already?" he teased.

Waving her red flag of challenge, she replied, "Remind me." She was flushed and breathing hard, her chest rose and fell deeply, and her nipples hardened.

"You are mine to do with as I see fit."

He inched closer until his nose almost touched hers. Rachael forgot all her smart quips and comebacks and, for a moment, did a good impression of a bunny caught in headlights. She wanted to feel his mouth on hers and to experience the unique pleasure of his kiss. She closed the gap, entwining one arm around his neck and the other over his shoulder for support. She brushed her lips over his then increased the pressure, slipping her tongue inside his mouth as he yielded. Time became irrelevant. She had no idea how long they kissed that way, but at some point Joshua leaned over to one side and, without breaking the kiss, rolled and pulled her on top of him. She had forgotten just how wonderful a good kiss could be—full of promise and anticipation. When they finally eased apart, she opened her eyes and found herself afloat in a vision of sky blue. His passion-heavy lids lent a sexy intensity to his gaze as he looked deeply into her eyes. She felt a pressure in her chest that she couldn't explain, almost as if she were going to cry, such was the level of emotion. It frightened her. It consumed her.

* * * *

Oh, man! Her lips tasted like sweet, swollen grapes ready for harvest, and her kiss intoxicated him as much as the resulting wine. He needed to think straight, although at that precise moment he couldn't think why. That was it—if he didn't move away now, they'd never leave his room. *What's so bad about that?* With a considerable effort that tested his strength of character to the limit, he backed off the bed, carefully hiding the sudden desire he had to tell her that he loved her. He thought that such a declaration might just scare her a little. It sure scared the hell out of him.

"If that is your opening act, I may not survive the play." She chuckled softly.

"Well, the main scene may just be a showstopper." He winked playfully. "*But,* as much as I want to spend all our time in bed, I am trying to behave and...court you."

He felt a bit embarrassed. He was great at coaxing cattle and horses but could count on both thumbs the times he'd actually wooed a woman. She must have guessed because she immediately tried to put him at ease.

"It's okay. I like that. I appreciate it, and, as you said earlier, this morning, it's just us." She smiled warmly at him. "It's a good thing to get to know each other." Then, to lighten the mood, she added, "I confess, though, the part about being in bed all day sounded pretty good, too." She held out her hand, and he pulled her off the bed. "Anyway, you did promise to cook for me, and you wouldn't want me to feel shortchanged now, would you?"

No, he certainly would not. Holding Rachael's hand, Joshua led her back to the kitchen where two still-cold beers waited for them. They found James and Janet lazing in the comfy chairs on the back deck that extended out from the veranda.

"I'm just going to call Colin about Crossling's horse." She backed away with her cell.

Joshua explained to the others what had happened that morning. When Rachael snapped her phone shut, she looked troubled.

"Colin said that the horse is doing well, but he wants to keep him longer under observation, just in case. Roy, however, is insisting on the horse going back to his place tonight. Somewhere, there's a village missing an idiot."

"It sounds as if you did all you could. It's his horse, unfortunately. He's a tight bastard. Probably didn't want to pay the extra fee." James grimaced.

"You've had an interesting day," Janet observed. "And it's only halfway through."

"Speaking of interesting, I see that the deputy got you home in one piece," Rachael teased.

"What do you mean? Did Mitch take you home last night?" James looked concerned.

"Yeah, what of it? Don't you approve of Mitch?" Janet challenged.

"Oh, he's a great guy, as a *friend*. He's too…big for anything else."

Joshua understood James's concern. Being the oldest, he'd had a few awkward conversations with Janet as she'd grown up, but he was damned if he was going to discuss *that*. Anyway, judging by the pink now creeping into her checks, he didn't have to.

"I'm well aware how tall and broad he is. That's part of his appeal. I fail to see why it's a problem or why you should be concerned."

She wasn't letting on what she did or didn't know and Joshua was okay with that. He'd realized last night that she was a grown woman and needed some privacy. James, on the other hand, hadn't cottoned on to the fact.

"Just brotherly concern, munchkin." James sighed.

"Don't call me that! I appreciate it, but you may want to remember that those lovely ladies that you entertain on a frequent basis are probably someone's sister too."

"Yeah, but they're someone *else's*."

Rachael and Janet couldn't help but laugh at James's double standards.

"If you must know, Josh asked Mitch to give me a lift home last night."

"Really? Well, that was decent of the deputy, and I'm sure that he behaved himself, right?" he said, fishing. "Josh, what do you think about this?"

"I think that I'm cooking tonight," Joshua announced. He wasn't about to get drawn into a family argument, not this afternoon.

"Great! You're in for a treat, Rachael. My big brother makes a mean stew." Janet beamed.

When she thought that he wasn't looking, she pulled her tongue out at James.

"I make other things too," he pointed out, because stew didn't seem that impressive.

"Yeah, but your stew is to die for. Please make that tonight. Go on, I've not had your stew since I was home last term," Janet pleaded.

He looked at Rachael, and she shrugged. "Stew sounds good to me. Can I help with the preparation?"

"Sure, we'll get started now, and it'll be an early dinner." He leaned in closer to Rachael and spoke so that only she could hear. "I want to be finished well before sundown so that I can see your naked body bathed in golden light."

"You really do have a creative side," she murmured back.

They made a good team in the kitchen. Rachael busied herself peeling and chopping vegetables while Joshua handled the steak, herbs and spices. He noted her skill with the knife. She was pretty nifty dicing and slicing. Come to think of it, perhaps she should be the one cutting the meat, considering her job and all.

"So, you cook most Sundays?"

"I used to before Janet went to college. I guess it was a way of keeping us together and following on from what our parents used to do. When she's not home, and it's just James and me, I don't always bother."

"Sounds like a good tradition. Is that your own beef you're cutting?"

"'Yep, Sweet Water steak—the best."

They moved easily around each other while attending to their tasks. She stopped suddenly when she noticed that he had paused and was watching her.

"What?"

"You were singing."

"Oh, was I?"

"Yeah, sounded—happy."

"Well, I guess I am." She smiled, looking mildly surprised.

He stepped closer to her. "And, now, so am I." He leaned down and kissed her softly and sweetly, not just a lovers' kiss but a loving one, too.

"I think I like being wooed," she chuckled.

He liked wooing her, but he couldn't stand it any longer. Being in close proximity to her was driving him crazy. His good intentions of not taking her until sunset were fading fast. When they finished preparing the meal, he knew that he didn't want to wait any longer to be inside her again. She was like a drug, and he was addicted.

"Rachael," his voice sounded like moving gravel, "go and get changed into your skirt and come to the back veranda. Leave your panties off."

She stared at him for a moment, biting her bottom lip, before heading to his room without saying a word.

Joshua waited alone. Janet and James were obviously trying to be discreet and give them some space. When Rachael appeared looking beautiful and feminine in a long, nearly ankle-length peasant skirt, his cock began to stir.

"You look lovely, darlin'. I want to show you the garden."

"Really? And that's why I'm not wearing knickers, is it?"

"Well, there may be a break in the tour."

"I think you're just leading me down the garden path."

He did take her down the garden path and over a small stream. After about ten minutes, they came to a clearing were a large tree stood with a low wooden swing attached to one of its huge limbs. It looked magical.

"Have a seat," he said.

"I've not sat in a swing for over fifteen years. It's sad, actually, when you think of all the little pleasures we dismiss as adults." She began to gently swing. "Did you use this as a kid?"

"Yeah, there's been a swing here for generations."

"I think it must be reassuring to have a history and attachment to a place like this. That's why I love my little cabin so much."

Joshua slowed the swing down and moved in front of Rachael. Without saying a word, he pushed her legs apart and knelt between them. Just as he'd thought, the swing was low enough and he was tall enough to facilitate a good fucking. He pushed his jeans a little way down, effectively freeing his erect shaft. Still not speaking, he trailed his fingers along her thigh, while he unselfconsciously stroked himself with his other hand. When his fingers reached the apex of her legs, he was unsurprised to feel swollen, moist, soft folds.

Knowing that she was ready for him, he bunched up her skirt and positioned the head of his cock within the lips of her warm pussy. Needing no verbal instruction, Rachael wrapped her legs loosely around his waist and held on tightly to the rope. He gripped the edges of the swing seat with each hand and swung it forward, which caused his cock to be buried deep inside her.

She gasped as he filled and stretched her like a big hand in a small latex glove. She leaned farther back on the swing to give an even deeper angle of penetration as he repeatedly rocked her onto his cock. He could clearly see his length slipping into her cunt. It looked like burst, ripe fruit split around his width. She also brazenly watched the erotic sight for a little while before gazing intently into his eyes with a look of desire and devilment. She purposely squeezed and clenched her pussy, clasping even tighter around him. His eyes widened at the unexpected exquisite sensation. Rachael groaned as she then reversed the action of her muscles, pushing out, as if trying to expel him.

"Jesus, what are you doing?" he ground out as his whole body thrummed with pleasure at the unsurpassed stimulation of his cock.

"Fucking you."

Again and again, she clenched her muscles tight, clutched his straining, taut shaft with a warm, slick, vice-like grip, drew him deeper inside, then released and pushed forcefully. Her muscles squeezed around his cock and pressed against his hard flesh.

He stopped moving, holding Rachael and the swing close to his body and gave in to the escalating waves of sheer pleasure.

"Come for me, Joshua," she commanded, wrapping her legs tighter around him.

Unable and unwilling to fight against the climax building, he erupted into her, expelling a loud grunt as he spurted his release, surrendering his seed into her silken embrace.

He wrapped his arms around her waist and, burying his head in her hair, caught his breath. Then he did something he'd never done before after sex— he started to chuckle.

"Hell, woman, you are full of surprises."

"Just giving you a taste of your own medicine." She giggled along with him.

As he came down slowly from the sexual high, he realized that not only had he never laughed after sex, he had never let a women take control either. He knew it now, clear as a fresh mountain lake: he loved her. He drew back and looked at her in wonderment. He had thought that he only wanted to dominate, but Rachael had turned the tables on him, and he had enjoyed it.

"Speaking of a taste, I believe I owe you one. You didn't come."

She grinned. "If we are keeping score, then I'm well up on the orgasm chart. Anyway, I've got a sneaking suspicion you'll make up for it later."

He nodded as he produced a clean neckerchief from his pocket. "At least let me clean you up."

She began to protest, but he silenced her with a kiss as his hand caressed between her legs, cleaning the evidence of their union.

"You're doing a very thorough job," she murmured, breaking the kiss for a second.

"I've a good work ethic."

He teased her a little, playing with her clit, but not settling into the rhythm required to take her over the edge. She moaned into his mouth as he deepened the kiss. "Please, Joshua."

He stopped. "Later. I'll make it up to you later. Come on. We'd better check on dinner."

She huffed and pouted, but she didn't protest. It was darn cute.

Joshua smiled to himself, a little teasing helped to raise the game. He would give her what she deserved a little later, no doubt about that.

Chapter 6

James and Janet had already set the table, and they all sat down to a casual dinner at 6:00 p.m.

"Gosh, you weren't kidding. This stew is great," Rachael commented after her first delicious mouthful. Joshua looked pleased as he sipped his wine.

It was clear to Rachael that Joshua's siblings were delighted to be entertaining her, and she couldn't help but feel completely at home in their company. She told them about her family and, in particular, the escapades of her two brothers. After one particularly funny story, Janet was crying with laughter, holding her sides.

"Oh, oh, it can't be true," she gasped.

"I swear to God, the car ended down a trench. They didn't know it was there because workmen had only dug it the day before."

"Your brothers sound like a lot of fun." James chuckled.

"You may meet them soon. I think they'll use the excuse of a family visit to look at the possibility of moving back themselves. It shouldn't be too difficult for them to find work in the oil industry here because they work in oil and gas exploration in the North Sea at the moment."

"Perhaps they can send us a CV," James suggested.

"Why?" Rachael asked. "They don't know much about cattle."

James and Janet looked confused. Frowning, they glanced at each other and then at Joshua.

"We aren't only a cattle ranch. We have other business concerns, primarily petroleum."

She wondered why he had neglected to mention it when they were talking over lunch.

"That must keep you busy," she said casually.

It hurt a little to think that he may have deliberately skirted around telling her about his business when she had been so open about herself. She recovered quickly from the embarrassment she felt in front of his brother and sister at obviously knowing so little about his life. The situation brought it home to her that she had known him less than one week. Here she was having unprotected, rampant sex with a virtual stranger. It wasn't her at all. She just didn't do this sort of thing! She took a big gulp of her wine.

"Very busy in the early days," he answered. "But now we have managers to handle the day-to-day running of the company. It allows me to be involved more with the ranch, which I enjoy. James deals with the engineering and technical side of things."

"Actually, Joshua, I want to speak to you about that. I think that once my exams are over I want to become more actively involved," Janet said, giving Rachael a wink. She then abruptly changed the subject. "But let's not talk about business now. Do you think you'll stay in Meadow Ridge, Rachael?"

Janet, bless her, had realized that she was uncomfortable and had redirected the conversation. "Well, I've only been here a week, although it seems much longer somehow. It is still early days, but I really feel like I've come home." She sighed, frowning. "I know it sounds weird..."

"No, not at all." Janet squeezed her hand. "You were born here. You have family history and ties to this place. You're a part of this land. I hope that you decide to stay, that's for sure." She started to giggle. "Gosh, I'm just remembering what you said to Roy."

Rachael was thankful for Janet's thoughtfulness and her light, bubbly nature. "Thanks for saying that. I appreciate it." She gave Janet a hug.

"Wow, female bonding, I've never seen it before, it—it—brings tears to my eyes," James choked out, pretending to wipe away a tear.

Janet and Rachael both laughed and simultaneously swatted him.

"I'm off. I will not be manhandled in this manner," James huffed. "Not by my sister, anyway." He caught Joshua's glare and quickly added, "And not by you, either, Rachael." As James rose from his seat, Rachael caught the slight jerk of his head that he aimed at Janet. "Thank you for the fine meal, brother, but I think I shall retire to the comfort of the TV room."

"Oh, I'll join you," Janet rushed to say. "Thanks for dinner, Josh. See you later, Rachael." She skipped after James.

"They are lovely. Not too subtle, though," Rachael sighed.

"They like you."

"I like them."

"I'm sorry that I didn't mention about the oil business. It didn't seem particularly relevant, and I don't like to shout about it. It has sometimes made a difference in how people behave. I guess that we haven't taken the time to do all the usual fact- and fiction-finding that goes on in a relationship."

"We'd better be careful. Hot sex can lead to meaningful conversation," she said, half joking. She should have felt annoyed, but to be honest, she understood his position. "Look, I don't care about what you do. No—that's not right—of course I care because it's what *you* do. What I mean is it doesn't change the way I feel."

"And how's that?" He was watching her intently.

Shit, had she really just said that? Damn, but the wine must have weakened her guard.

"That I want more...of you," she said quietly, surprised by her own candidness.

"I was just thinking the same thing." He stood up and walked around to her side of the table. Standing behind her with his hands on her shoulders, he leaned over and kissed her neck.

"I'm going to give you much more. Come with me," he murmured in her ear as he pulled back her chair and took her hand in his.

He led her to his wing of the house and the bedroom. It was nearly a quarter to eight, and the sun was low on the horizon.

"Take off your clothes," he told her and stepped back to watch as he started to unbutton his own shirt.

As she had no panties on, she left the skirt until last, letting it float to the floor. They stood side by side, naked, watching the sky as the soft hues of orange, red, and yellow light flooded the landscape and the room. Then they turned to each other with open appraisal and saw that, for those few moments, they were unearthly beautiful creatures of light touched by the last rays of the dying day.

"Have you ever been taken in the ass before, Rachael?" he asked quietly, somehow making the words seem less blunt, crude, and embarrassing. He carefully watched her, waiting for an answer.

Uh oh. The peaceful feeling disappeared fast, like the golden light of the sun now dropping over the edge of the world being replaced by the muted shades of apprehension.

"N–no."

"Get on your back, Rachael. Spread your legs, and raise your knees." His voice was tightly controlled and devoid of feeling.

She hesitated, chills traversing her spin and ribs.

"Thinking of backing out?"

"No," she said clearly and defiantly.

She gracefully crawled on to the bed and turned over on to her back, bending her knees as directed. It felt so sluttish and rude to openly display herself in this way, but, God, what a turn on, too. Joshua fished out two pairs of velvet-lined, leather handcuffs from the bedside cabinet. Rachael watched as if hypnotized by them. Each leather cuff was attached to another by a thin, adjustable silver chain. He worked silently with purpose. First, he tied one cuff to her right wrist and the corresponding cuff to her right ankle; then, he adjusted the chain so that she would not be able to straighten her leg or move her arm very far. He then repeated the exercise with her left wrist and leg. When he finished, she was effectively restrained. This was all new for Rachael, and her body hummed with delicious, tightly coiled sexual tension. She realized that her imaginative mind was an erogenous zone of epic proportions and Joshua was feeding the fantasy, making her feel hornier than ever before. She wanted to wrap her legs around him and impale herself on his cock, but she couldn't. The waiting and anticipation frayed her senses, stripping away anxiety and leaving only a raw desire.

He placed a pillow under her butt to raise it higher, and stepped back to get a good look at her.

"I'm going to take your ass, Rachael. It'll be easier on you in this position. The initial entry will be less tight and more comfortable for you than if you were on all fours."

He moved between her legs and applied copious amounts of lube to his cock and her ass and pushed some of the cold jell into her hot channel. As he pressed the head of his cock to her sphincter, it twitched and tightened.

"Joshua, I'm worried. You're a big man."

"You have to relax, love," he soothed. "I'll go real slow, trust me. I'll fit like a hand in a glove."

Suddenly a vision of the O.J. Simpson trial came into her mind. One size doesn't always fit all. She stifled a nervous giggle.

"Now, take a deep breath and let it out slowly," he coaxed.

She had to simply lie back and let it happen. The cuffs prevented much movement. She trusted him with her body and hoped that he wouldn't let her down. When she did as he bid, he pressed the slippery head of his cock against her and gently, steadily pushed forward, parting the portal to her virgin hole. *Oh, my.*

"You're doing great, Rachael. Just relax, love. I'm nearly in."

He was very careful, slowly and steadily pressing forward. All the time, he watched her face.

"Breathe, darlin', and try to relax," he coaxed in anguished chords.

As his flared cockhead pushed through, opening the tightly closed entrance muscles, Rachael almost panicked. It felt as if he were stretching and filling her beyond her capacity.

"I'm in."

The unpleasant sensation eased and she simply felt incredibly full. He carefully inched deeper in small, pulsing increments. All the while, his face was a picture of concentration and restraint. He kissed her softly, parting her lips, lightly pushing his tongue into her mouth in time to the motion of his hips. When he withdrew his tongue, she pushed hers into his mouth and began to dictate the pace. She started gently and slowly, and he followed the rhythm with his thrusts in her ass.

Her body adjusted, and she soon she wanted more. She picked up the pace with her tongue, tilted her hips and moaned her pleasure. It must have convinced him that she was asking for more because he thrust faster and deeper. It was exquisite.

He broke the kiss and leaned back to gain access to her pussy with his hand. When he stuck two fingers into her wet depths, she cried out. He played with her clit, rubbing, lightly pinching the hood back between his finger and thumb. Locking the screams in her throat, she still couldn't prevent the mewing noises that escaped.

"You don't have to be quiet, Rachael. No one will hear you here except me. Don't fight it, darlin', I want to hear your pleasure," he groaned.

She panted. "I'm so close, so close."

She pictured climbing a tower and reaching the top, the rickety structure wobbling and swaying, and then the inevitable collapsing, cascading down as wave after wave of molten hot pleasure swamped her. She screamed his name and thrashed beneath him as he dug himself to the hilt. She felt her passage tighten around him. He sucked in a breath.

"Fuck. Stay still, Rachael, I don't want to blow just yet. There's more."

More? What more? But even as she thought it, she wanted it.

He stared at her with such lust and longing that she wondered if she had conjured up a neon sign over her head saying, "Fuck me any way you want to."

With what must have been supreme self-control, he waited for her orgasm to subside before withdrawing his still-erect cock.

"Now that you're stretched, I'm going to take that ass of yours the way I want to. Roll over and get on your knees."

His gentle, tender tone had been replaced by a cold, commanding one. In a dreamlike, passion-induced state, she found herself again complying, but due to the restraints, she couldn't rest on her hands, only her shoulders.

"Spread your thighs. Raise your butt. Prepare to be mounted and ridden hard."

Oh, my God. His roughly spoken words fueled the fantasy and heightened her lust. She felt submissive yet sexy, degraded yet desired. She saw him grit his teeth, close his eyes for a second, and settle himself. He applied more lubrication into her ass, lathered the puckered opening, and pushed the cold gel gently inside. This time, he pressed his slippery, hard length slowly but more forcefully through the tight ring of muscle. The angle of her body amplified his size, and she suddenly snapped out of the passion fugue. It was not comfortable. The sensation of pain seamed with pleasure hovered in the erotic no man's land between the two. She took a sharp breath, and he stopped.

"It feels almost too much. You're so big, but it feels good. I–I don't know if…" She moaned.

He stopped for a moment to let her relax, to give her body and mind time to adjust.

"You'll take it all because you want more." He sounded harsh with lust.

He moved gently at first, slowly building up the pace.

"You're a naughty girl, Rachael. You like it up the ass, don't you?"

When she didn't answer, he slapped her buttocks, then grabbed her hips and pulled her firmly onto his shaft.

"Answer me."

"Yes," she hissed, her synapses snapping, overwrought with a need too great to contain.

"Do you still want more? Do you want me to fuck this sweet hole full of come?"

"Yes." Her voice quavered, and she was on the verge of the mother of all orgasms.

"Good. That's what I'm going to do."

He reached around her waist, strummed her clit, pushed three fingers into her pussy, and moved them in time with his thrusting hips. He grunted and bucked harder as she jerked and thrashed, his substantial scrotum slapping her twat and thighs. With her face turned to one side, she could see the scene reflected in the mirror. Rachael lost control. Her hips convulsed, and she slammed back against him, driving his cock deep to the hilt. As she howled her climax, he gave a warriors guttural roar and released his warm load deep within her with forceful, streaming pulses.

They stilled, locked together, breathing hard, unable to form coherent speech. Staying buried balls deep, Joshua leaned over and undid her wrist cuffs. She pushed up onto her hands, arching and stretching out her spine like a contented, satisfied cat, snuggling her butt into his groin. He stroked her back, breasts and sides. She reached between her legs and caressed his sac.

After several minutes, Rachael looked over her shoulder and smiled mischievously. She was suddenly feeling playful and energized.

"You were right about your performance being a showstopper. I can't wait for the encore, although I doubt I'll survive it." She giggled.

"Encore? You're already thinking about an encore? Jesus, I doubt I'll survive *you*."

They both grinned. He sighed and cuddled closer to her.

"Thank you," she said softly, with serious sincerity. "It was amazing, and you made me feel," she wanted to say loved, "special."

He blinked, looking delighted and mildly surprised. "Thank you, too, and you are."

He slowly withdrew from her body and went to the bathroom. She waited her turn to do the same. When she emerged, she found him looking gorgeous and relaxed, reclining on the bed with his hands clasped behind his head. She straddled his hips as she sat in his lap and leaned down to trail kisses from his collarbone, up his neck, on his cheeks, nose and, finally, his mouth. She honestly felt that she would never get enough of the taste and smell of him, and she certainly couldn't imagine getting bored.

"You know, I didn't have any dessert this evening," he said with a gleam in his eye. "I want some pie."

Rachael understood. She raised herself on her knees and off his lap a little to allow him to shuffle down the bed between her thighs. Then holding onto the headboard, she lowered herself onto his face.

"I'm sorry, sir, but we only have cream with our pie," she teased, knowing that her pussy was wet again.

"My favorite," he mumbled, then swiped along her slit, lapping up her juices. "It's fucking ambrosia."

He focused on her clit, flicking and swirling with his warm, wet, talented tongue, applying the perfect pressure. Within moments, Rachael was close to orgasm again. As she started to shudder and writhe, he grabbed her thighs to hold her in place.

"Oh, my God. Oh, my God. It's too much," she cried as her climax crashed down upon her and her pussy muscles rippled in surrender to overstimulated nerve endings. He slowed but didn't stop. It was exquisite torture. She tried to pull away but he held her fast. Her clit was supersensitive. Every touch sent a spasm through her cervix into her womb and radiating outwards, flooding her body with a fire-and-ice sensation too intense to bear.

"No!" she screamed, finally ripping herself out of his grip and falling to the side.

He rolled on top of her and kissed her savagely, cutting off her protest. His face was wet with her juices, and she could taste her own essence. Urgently, he prized her legs apart and abruptly plunged his wide, long and, yet again, hard cock deep into her up to the hilt, nudging the neck of her womb.

"Yes! Fuck me," she pleaded.

He obliged, wildly pounding into her. It was a primitive, frenzied fucking. She raised her hips, lunging into his thrusts, urging him on, needing him to fill her throbbing channel. Another climax erupted, bursting out from deep within her core. He thrust hard one, two, three more times before he reared up and an orgasm dragged yet more come from his balls. Rachael wrapped her strong legs tightly around him and held him close as her internal muscles continued to massage his thrumming shaft.

Panting, he collapsed on her, his hard muscles gleaming with sweat. After a few minutes, she pushed gently on his chest, and he shifted his weight to the side.

"Jesus, Ryden, just how much sperm do these puppies produce?" Rachael laughed breathlessly in post-orgasmic bliss while fondling his bollocks.

"I really don't know. We should conduct intensive field tests." He chuckled into her soft curly hair.

"Oh, no, you don't. It's past midnight, so you don't call the shots anymore, and I would like to be able to walk tomorrow."

He suddenly looked worried. "Did I hurt you?"

"No, but I know what one of your heifers feel like." She yawned and started to get up.

Joshua's eyes narrowed. "What are you doing?"

"Er, getting up to go home," she said uncertainly, aware that he didn't look pleased.

"What do you think this is all about Rachael? Do you think it's only sex to me? Is it only a good fuck to you?" He sounded cold.

"No, but I didn't want to assume....do you want me to stay the night and sleep with you?"

"Yes."

"Okay, then, don't get your knickers in a twist. I'd love to sleep over with you. Just know this: if you snore, you'll feel my elbow." She bounced back down on the bed, feeling something akin to jubilation but trying not to show it. Joshua smiled at her indulgently.

They snuggled beneath the crisp cotton covers, and Rachael felt secure and cosseted with Joshua's big body spooned around hers. Her eyelids became heavy and she drifted off. He murmured something that sounded like "I love you," but she didn't really register the words and soon they were both enshrouded in the soft cloak of slumber.

* * * *

At six o'clock in the morning, Joshua's alarm on his watch beeped irritatingly. He had forgotten to reset it. Five seconds later, it was followed by Rachael's.

"It's a conspiracy," Rachael grumbled into the pillow.

Joshua unfolded himself from around her warm body after the best night's sleep he'd had in a long time. He reached for both their watches and cancelled the persistent bleeps.

He brushed her shoulder with his lips and enjoyed the feel and sight of her in his bed. *I could get used to this.*

"Good morning, beautiful."

She sighed sleepily and snuggled back against him, pulling his arm tighter around her. Suddenly she stilled. He'd been discovered.

"Are you looking for something beneath the sheets because that's got to be a torch, right?"

"Sorry, sweetheart, but that's how it is in the morning—it's just very happy to see you."

"I'm surprised that it's not shriveled in exhaustion waving a white flag."

"No, darlin'. Never around you. In fact, I'd say it wants to make a fresh assault."

Without being told, Rachael stayed on her side but moved her top leg forward, arched her back, and pressed her butt farther against his erection. He felt her slick readiness with a hand dipped between her thighs and simply surged into her heavenly depths. Home, he was home. This time, it was a slow, unhurried pace, and afterwards they both drifted back off to sleep with Joshua still inside.

An hour later, he stirred and pulled her to his chest in a tender embrace. He leaned down, buried his face in her hair, and breathed in her fragrance. It was as if she had cast a spell on him. He felt different when she was near. He sensed that he was becoming a part of something, yet, at the same time, had never felt so whole.

"I have to go to Houston for a few days. I'm leaving at eleven. You don't need to rush, but let's have breakfast before I leave. I feel really hungry."

"I can't think why that would be. God, you're as horny as a teenager." She chuckled.

They showered together, making a more than thorough job of it. Afterward they chatted lightly as they dressed and then left the room.

Out of the blue, a question left his lips. "I know that you're good with animals, but what about children?" Even he was surprised. *Where the hell did that come from?* He hadn't given a lot of thought to the whole family issue in the past, but in the last few days, it has surfaced in his mind.

"Goodness, when I warned that sex could lead to meaningful conversation, I was actually joking, but, hey, you asked for it. I like kids. I'd love a posse of them, to be honest." She stared at him, waiting for a reaction. He was a little surprised and a lot pleased.

She grinned. "That's odd. I was at least expecting skid marks as you ran for the hills. I thought you'd be terrified."

"No, not at all, but I am surprised. I thought that your career would come first."

"You know, people change, they grow, and their circumstances alter. It provides endless possibilities on the direction a life can take. I love my work. It is one of the most important things to me aside from my family, but if I am still doing exactly the same thing in the same way in five years time, I'll be disappointed. I think we have to move forward and experience as much of this God-given gift of a life as we can. I'll be happy to have a change when the time and situation is right. How's that for a bit of philosophy at seven thirty in the morning. What about you?"

"Me?" He held the door to the main part of the house open for her. "The more, the merrier I say, and I'd enjoy the practicing in the meantime."

She giggled. "Well, you shouldn't have any difficulty. What with bollocks like an everlasting porridge pot."

He burst out laughing. Janet and James were having breakfast and stopped to look at each other and then at him with mild surprise. It was far too long since they'd last heard that hearty sound from his lips.

"Good morning," Rachael sang as she sauntered to the table. "Any coffee going?"

"Sure." Janet waved at the coffeepot on the table. "Help yourself."

"Isabella is making pancakes." James grinned at them both. "Better get your order in."

Joshua strolled into the kitchen while Rachael sat down. He greeted Isabella and swiped a stack of pancakes piled on a plate, which he placed in the center of the table.

"First batch. Dig in."

As they ate breakfast, Rachael offered to take him to the airport since she had to go into town to stock up on food supplies and get some household stuff for her new home. Janet, a self-confessed snoop, invited herself over to Rachael's cabin on Tuesday night for dinner.

"You know, our family has always wanted that land of yours, but generations of your mama's would never let it go."

"Really? Well, I'll be honest, I won't be the one to break tradition. Do you like Italian? We'll have pasta, wine, and watch a girlie flick. How about that?"

"Oh, sounds great. There's too much testosterone around here. I'd love a girls' night in!"

"So would I." James looked hopeful.

"Sorry, bro, but that penis in your pants is an automatic bar."

"That's sexual discrimination, that is."

"Yeah, get used to it." Janet smirked.

Joshua rolled his eyes. "I'll go get my stuff and we'll head off."

He wished that he didn't have to go, but he had a lot of meetings planned and decisions that needed to be made. He'd considered asking Rachael to go with him but couldn't afford to be distracted on this trip, and he would hardly have any time to spend with her. Still, he didn't really need that much sleep...no, he had to be sharp and quick for the sake of the business.

As they arrived at the airport, Joshua directed Rachael to drive away from the main building toward the aircraft hangars, and he made a phone call.

"Hello, Mac. I'm here...Is it prepped and ready to go?...Great, see you in a minute."

Rachael looked at him with an eyebrow cocked and a sardonic twist to her mouth.

He sighed. "Yep, we have a company jet."

"I bet you fly it, too."

"Sometimes. If I'm not too busy working on the way."

"You really are multitalented." And in usually Rachael fashion, she got right to the point. "How come you're single? I'm thinking secret alter ego, axe murderer, or something."

He regarded her sternly for a moment, then snorted, "You are direct, and I could ask you the same question."

"I've never met that special person who I want to annoy for the rest of my life," she joked. "I asked first."

"It's been said that I'm arrogant, bossy, domineering, intimidating, controlling, and sexually rapacious and voracious, among other things. I've never met a woman who can handle that— handle me—until maybe...now."

Rachael absorbed his words and gave him a few of her own, "Honest, responsible, loyal, adventurous, challenging, sexy, masculine, intelligent, attractive, awesome in bed, among other things, and you're darn right about one thing—I can handle that."

He leaned over and kissed her hungrily on the lips. She managed to pull back, breathing hard.

"If you don't go now, I'm driving off with you to the nearest secluded place."

"That's kidnapping," he growled, thinking that it was a great idea.

"Man-napping, actually, and it'll be a hostage situation. I can promise you that, so get out now." She was gripping the steering wheel.

"I will be back on Thursday. Get plenty of rest Wednesday night."

"Follow your own advice. I'll see you then."

He started to get out.

"Oh," she added, "and I'll be working on my poker skills."

Implausibly, his cock became even harder. Thursday couldn't come soon enough.

Chapter 7

Rachael spent the rest of the day stocking up on supplies and buying stuff that she needed for the cabin. She popped into the Vet Practice to inquire about Crossling's horse. Colin was out, but Sandy, his shy new receptionist, greeted her warmly. When Rachael asked about the horse, Sandy's face dropped.

"It was fine when Roy took him away, but two hours ago he rang to say that it had died in the night. Colin went over there to see for himself. He should be back soon."

"I can't believe it. Do you know why?"

"No, Roy wouldn't give any details but he's—he's blaming you." She looked embarrassed and worried.

"What? I saved that horse's life. It wouldn't have made it back here if I hadn't opened its airways. This is terrible news. I don't understand it. Poor horse."

Just then, Colin's truck swung into the reserved space next to Rachael's Jeep, and Rachael ran out to meet him. He looked pissed off.

"Sandy has just filled me in. Do you know what happened?"

"Not really. Not the full story, anyway. Crossling won't let me see the horse. He says it died last night, and he's buried it. It's damned suspicious, Rachael." He raked his fingers through his hair. "He said he thinks that you did something wrong and is currently deciding whether to take the matter further."

"No way," Rachael spat. "Not without a body and an autopsy. What was the condition of the horse when he left you?"

"Fine, although, like I said yesterday, I would have liked to have had him under observation a bit longer. I administered the antivenin in time and, because you'd managed to keep the swelling and any infection under control early on, I really thought he was okay."

"Crossling is angry because I insulted him. He's doing this to spread gossip about me and harm my professional reputation. We need to do some damage control and insist on seeing the corpse."

No matter what they did, Roy Crossling wouldn't let them onto his property. Even when they took a police officer along to the ranch, they couldn't persuade him.

"He's within his legal rights." Officer McGowan shrugged. "In the eyes of the law, he hasn't done anything wrong."

"What about slander?"

"Well, that's a civil private matter, and he hasn't done it openly yet. The problem is that he doesn't really need to because news travels fast here. I'm sorry."

Rachael felt a cold sense of dread creep over her.

"We just need to spread the truth then," Colin said. "I need to make a few calls."

That evening Rachael went to bed early and had restless dreams about Joshua, snakes, and horses.

In the morning, she still felt tired but tried to put Crossling out of her mind. *The truth will win in the end.* Mid-afternoon, she got a call from Colin, and it wasn't good news. He hadn't heard anymore from Crossling, but the American Medical Veterinary Association had contacted him because he was her sponsor. Apparently, they had received a complaint that Rachael was practicing without a Texan license and the death of an animal had been mentioned. Colin had carefully explained the circumstances and lack of any evidence, including a corpse. The man had been sympathetic but stressed that the Association had procedures that must be followed, and her license would, at best, be delayed while the matter was investigated.

"Do you want to come over for dinner? I don't want you to worry alone."

"Thanks, Colin, but I'm having Janet Ryden over for a girls' night in."

"Good, well, have fun and keep me posted if you hear anything more."

Janet arrived at seven with a chilled bottle of Sauvignon Blanc.

"Let's open it straight away and drown my sorrows. You'll never guess what's been going on."

Rachael told Janet all about the false accusation and her concern about her future career in Texas.

"Roy's a spineless little rat. Damn, I'm sorry that you got involved. If you hadn't helped me—"

"Now, hold on a minute. You can't blame yourself. It's squarely in his court."

"Yeah, but there have been bad feelings between our families for some time now. You see, thirty years ago, Roy's father was in a lot of financial trouble. He owed money to the bank and was about to get his property repossessed, so he asked our dads for help. They knew that he wasn't reliable, but they didn't want to see the family lose their land either, so they entered into a legal agreement. We leased a large area of their land and obtained the mineral rights for fifty years. Our daddies thought that there might be oil there, but it was a risk and they had to do a lot of exploration. Anyway, they found oil on Crossling's land and on our own, too. Of course, we started pumping on the leased land first. The Crosslings are hopping mad. They believe that the oil will all be gone before the lease runs out. That may or may not happen, and we are legally within our rights to suck it dry."

"I see, but that doesn't have much to do with me. He's just being bloody-minded. Here, have a top up." She poured more wine. "We'll watch *Love Actually*. How about that?"

"It sounds like a great plan."

"Speaking of love, how's things between you and the deputy?"

"Well, we have admitted our feelings for each other, and now I'm waiting for him to make the first move. He should be back from Austin by now, but I haven't heard from him. Maybe he's tired. What if he's changed his mind?" She looked horrified at the thought.

"Calm down, give him time. There's no way that man isn't interested in you."

"Rachael, he's had nine years. Okay, that's an exaggeration, but he'll miss his opportunity if he doesn't get his skates on. I'm going back to college in a few weeks."

"Well, maybe we can pick up a few tips from the big screen."

By the end of the movie, Rachael was ashamed to say she was definitely tipsy, but she was enjoying herself. Janet had only had two glasses of wine all evening and felt okay to drive home.

"You can stay here if you want to. There's a bed in the open loft."

"Thanks, but I promised I'd visit some of the wells early in the morning with James. I'm getting more involved in the business on somebody's good advice." She smiled. "Thanks again. It was a fun evening. Try not to worry too much about the whole horse thing. People aren't that stupid here. We'll make sure that the truth gets around."

"Thanks. Drive carefully now." Rachael gave Janet a hug and watched as the taillights of her car disappeared into the night. She hadn't liked to point out that it wasn't really gossip that was her primary concern. She was more worried about the prospect of her license being held up or, worse still, not granted.

Rachael went into the house and gave James a quick call to say that Janet was on her way home.

"Did you eat a tasty dinner, watch a good movie, and enjoy yourselves while I sat here on my lonesome?"

"Yes, we did, but the movie was a bit disappointing. *Hot Lesbian Vampires Do Dallas* wasn't half as good as we thought it was going to be. Good night, James." She quietly laughed to herself and got ready for bed.

* * * *

Janet drove carefully, avoiding the potholes and keeping alert for any animals that may have strayed onto the old country road. She was therefore surprised and a little worried when halfway home a flashing blue light appeared behind her and a short blast of a siren told her to pull over. *I wasn't speeding. I only had two glasses of wine and ate a full dinner. I'm not over the limit, surely.* Even so, she popped a mint into her mouth and crunched it down quickly in a guilty fashion, not quite knowing why she did it.

Gripping the steering wheel tightly, she watched in her rear view mirror as the hulking silhouette of a police officer came into view and alongside her SUV. He knocked on the window, blinding her with his torchlight. Squinting and shielding her eyes, she put the window down.

"Good evening, Officer. What's the problem?"

Still shining the light in her face, he said sternly, "Step out of the vehicle please, ma'am."

"Certainly, just as soon as you stop shining that torch in my eyes and show some ID."

"Step out of the vehicle now," the semi-recognizable voice repeated more harshly.

"I'm not going anywhere until you show me some ID. I know my rights." Actually, she didn't, but it sounded good. Her eyes were uncomfortable, and he was pissing her off.

Her door was tugged open, and she was pulled out faster than she thought possible. So much for her plan of holding on to the steering wheel.

The torch swung away from her face, and she was hauled around to the front of her SUV and was pushed against the hood.

"If you don't show me some ID right now, I'm getting back to my car," she said bravely, all the time feeling terrified.

She heard a deep laugh. "Spread 'em." He kicked her legs apart and placed her arms wide, holding her down easily with a big hand on the center of her back.

"What are you doing?" she shouted fearfully.

"Frisking you. Don't move."

"The hell I won't." She started to struggle in earnest.

"Shush, Janet. It's me, Mitch," he crooned softly into her ear as he leaned over her, holding her arms against the hood.

"Mitch? What are you playing at? Let me up." Her fear quickly morphed into relief, and she relaxed her tense stance.

"I'm being imaginative," he drawled.

"Ah, yes, about that—"

"Not so *cock* sure of yourself now, are you? Now stay still why I do my job."

She was so shocked that she complied, staying stock-still as he ran his hands firmly all over her. Jesus, if this was a normal frisk, she'd break the law every day. When he got to her chest, the efficient sweep became a lingering cup and squeeze. When he moved to her thighs, he placed his hand between her legs, flat against her sex, and rubbed back and forth. She couldn't help but moan. He pressed up against her, and she could feel the heat of his big body and the outline of his hard cock through his clothes. The sudden relief she had experienced now turned to raging desire.

He pulled her to stand upright, turned her around, and kissed her deeply, tasting her minty mouth.

"Have you been drinking?"

"N–no," she stammered. He narrowed his eyes. "Well, yes, just two glasses of wine with dinner." She'd never really mastered the art of lying. Joshua had never given her the chance.

"Walk in a straight line."

"What? Mitch! You know I'd never drive drunk."

"Just do it."

God, he sounded so different, sort of masterful, really. It was very sexy.

She sighed theatrically and walked in a dead-straight line and back again.

"I'm not convinced. Bend over and touch your toes."

"Now, Mitch, you're just being ridicul—ow!" He had smacked her bottom. She felt her pussy tremble as she slowly leaned forward. He unclipped his police baton and lifted her skirt with the end. She heard him hiss when he exposed her backside. She was only wearing a skimpy thong so she knew he was getting an eye full.

"Spread your legs wider. That's it, good girl."

This was a new side to the deputy—one she wasn't really prepared for, but ignited a longing for intimacy like she'd never experienced before.

* * * *

He stared at her almost bare ass, clad in a white lace thong. The pure but sexy look always did it for him. The urge to grab her hips and sink deep into her until he bounced against her full buttocks was fierce. Taking a steadying breath, he rubbed the end of the baton across her ass before sliding it on the fabric between her legs.

She stumbled forward.

"You look a little tipsy to me." He laughed softly.

Janet straightened and turned around. He moved in quickly, taking her in his arms and kissing her hard.

"I just wanted to get your attention," she murmured as he moved his mouth to her neck.

"You've got it, and you'll be getting a whole lot more in a minute." He felt her tremble against him as she tentatively ran her hands down his back to his butt.

"I want you, but you'll have to show me the way," she said demurely.

God, how did she know that the whole shy, virginal act turned him on?

His hand found its way under her skirt, his finger into her vagina. Lord, she was sopping but very tight. He'd never fit if she didn't relax. He carried her to the back of his police cruiser, opened the tailgate with one hand, and seated her on the edge.

"You need to relax, baby. I'm going conduct a thorough body search, starting here." He opened her legs wide and placed his hand on her mound. "I don't have a sniffer dog, so I'll have to do it myself." He wiggled his eyebrow and was pleased when she laughed. It would go some way to easing her nerves.

He gently directed her to lean back with her legs dangling over the edge of the tailgate. He could hardly believe it. Finally, Janet Ryden was spread open before him with just a thin piece of fabric between him and her heavenly snatch. He hunkered down with his face between her thighs and breathed hot breath through the fabric. She moaned and tilted her hips.

"Your panties are wet, sweetheart. Is this cream for me?"

"You know it is," she whispered. "I've waited for you."

Her declaration had him even hotter and harder for her. He'd also waited long enough to have her in his arms. He ripped the flimsy fabric, threw her torn panties to the ground, and slid a finger along her slippery opening and shallowly into her resistant flesh. Lord, she was tight. A small cry escaped her lips at the sudden invasion. It was replaced by a low moan when he dragged his tongue along the length of her folds. She was delicious, and he felt the blood pounding in his cock as he experienced her unique flavor for the first time. She tasted of warm woman, the ocean, spice, and something else unique to her and so right it had him desperate for her. He shook as he tried to control the tightening in his balls.

"I've thought about doing this for years. We're going to make up for lost time."

He heard her sharp intake of breath as he reached her clit and began to tickle it lightly with his wickedly mobile tongue.

"Mitch," she moaned.

"Do you want me, baby?"

"Yes, but I have tell you something," she panted.

"Don't worry, I've got protection."

He continued to massage her clit with his tongue. She began to squirm and small mewling sounds escaped her lips, along with his name. Possessive male satisfaction welled within him and he tongued her faster. She yelled into the night, shuddering as her core pelvic muscles rippled with her release.

Urgently, he pulled her upright and held her hand, directing it to his fly, which he had opened. In a dazed state, she hesitated for a fraction of a second, then reached between the folds of fabric. Her smooth warm hand touched his chunky, iron-hard erection. In response, his balls tightened and pre-cum seeped from the slit of his cock. She tried to encircle it with her hand but couldn't reach all the way around. He was wide.

"Take it out," he groaned and kissed her more deeply.

She cautiously released his cock. In the dim light cast by the glow of the tail lights, it looked as thick as her wrist. Her hand trembled in his as he guided her to help roll on a condom. "Don't worry. I'll go slow."

He knew that he was particularly wide, and some of his lovers had found it uncomfortable at first, but they'd all quickly come to appreciate it. He positioned the tip of his cock at her entrance and slid it back and forth to further lubricate it with her juices. She was wet and ready; he pressed forward. She was so tight, but her flesh began to relent.

"Mitch," she panted, "Mitch, I always wanted you to be the first."

He paused. "That's okay, sweetheart. We're here now." He chortled. "I'm not a virgin, either." He pushed a little harder, preparing to plow forward.

"I know you're not, but I am."

He froze. At exactly the same moment, he heard the sound of an engine and saw headlights appear over the hill.

"What?" His lust-fogged brain slowly processed the data: fuck, virgin, car, cover up.

He suddenly sobered up and quickly crammed his cock back into his pants, pulled down Janet's skirt, lifted her off the tailgate and slammed it shut. Who the hell was out on this road at this time of night?

"I'm sorry, I—" Janet stumbled over her words.

"Shh. No, sweetheart, no, don't say you're sorry. Don't apologize for that. I'm sorry. I didn't know." He hugged her to his big body and thanked God for the vehicle now approaching, because if it hadn't, he would have taken her there and then and none too gently, either. "I didn't listen to what you were trying to tell me. Jesus, Janet, your first time should be special."

"It would have been special because I'm with you." She sounded upset.

"I didn't mean it like that." He could tell she needed reassurance. "You will be with me, but for your first time, I want to be gentle. It'll be extra special for the both of us." His heart jumped a beat when he saw the way she looked at him with trust, love, and longing in her eyes. "You are so beautiful, Janet Ryden."

The vehicle that approached was slowing down. When the truck caught them in its headlights, it skidded to a stop on the other side of the road. Mitch flicked open his holster, just in case.

"Janet! Are you okay?" James shouted frantically.

He leapt out of his car, leaving his headlights on to see by and rushed over to them.

"James, I'm fine. What are you doing here?" Janet responded anxiously.

"Rachael rang nearly an hour ago to say that you were on your way. When you didn't arrive or answer your phone, I got worried. I thought you'd been involved in an accident. What have you been doing? Why are you stopped at the side of the road with the deputy?"

James started to calm down and take in the scene before him. Mitch knew what he was beginning to see—his sister and the deputy looking flustered and dishevelled. *This might not end well.*

"Mitch, what's going on?" James's tone became more serious.

"It's not what you think," Janet blurted out.

"Oh, really?" James, at first, looked amused, but his expression hardened as he spied something on the ground. "What—are—those?" He pointed to Janet's torn panties.

"I can explain." Mitch grimaced, doubting that he could do anything of the sort.

"You don't have to, Mitch." Janet stepped forward. "James, I don't need a lecture from a guy who has threesomes with his best friend and a different woman nearly every weekend."

James flinched.

She softened her voice. "I'm grateful that you love and care about me so much that you came out here, and I'm sorry that you got scared, but I'm okay. Really, I am. I love you, too, brother, but I'm a big girl now, so thank you but good night."

Both guys looked awkward. Mitch broke the silence.

"James, you should know how I feel about your sister. I would never hurt or use her. I love her." He turned to Janet. "Baby, technically I'm on a dinner break, and my patrol duty doesn't end until six a.m. How about you follow James home and I'll see you tomorrow night?"

When she looked as if she was about to protest, he maneuvered her farther away from James and whispered in her ear. "I want to do this right. Tomorrow, my work shift changes. We'll have a romantic evening in, just us. I'd like you to stay the night with me, in my bed, naked and satisfied. Does that sound okay?"

Janet nodded. "I wish it were tonight, but, yeah, that sounds great. I'll see you tomorrow." She turned back to James. "I'll follow you home now."

"Wait a minute. Walk in a straight line," James told her.

"What? Not you as well. I'm not drunk!"

"Please, just humor me."

Mitch wondered why James was paying particular attention to the way Janet walked. *No, surely he's not looking for signs of—damn, that Ryden boy sure was protective.* He didn't blame him.

Janet paced ten yards then back again. "See?"

"Just had to check. Maybe I overreacted. Just make sure that you do treat her right, Mitch."

Mitch nodded and James turned to head home, but didn't resist a parting comment.

"Oh, and, Deputy, do up your fly."

Fuck.

Chapter 8

The first thing Janet wanted to do when she woke up at 6:45 a.m. was to call Mitch. She knew that he had finished his night shift at 6:00 a.m. and should therefore still be awake. Sitting up in bed she dialed his number. He answered on the second ring.

"Hey, Janet. I was just thinking about you. I wasn't sure if you'd be awake yet so I planned on waiting until eight."

"Aren't you tired?"

"Yeah, but I wanted to speak to you before catching some Zs. Are you okay, babe?"

It was typical of Mitch to put her comfort before his own. He may look like a WWE wrestler, but he was all heart.

"I'm fine, although something interesting happened last night. I was stopped by a cop on my way home from Rachael's."

"Is that so?" He sounded amused.

"Yes. He was a big and mean and he made an inappropriate search of my person. It was police harassment. I'm thinking about laying charges." She fought hard to keep her voice level and not laugh.

"I'm thinking about laying you."

She giggled. "Me, too. It took me a while to get to sleep last night."

"I think that I'm gonna have the same problem. Look, I'll call you later this afternoon about tonight."

"Okay. Sweet dreams."

She was thrilled at the prospect of seeing him and of finally being with him. At least today she could keep herself busy so that the time would pass quickly.

Next, Janet called Joshua. She wanted to tell him about Rachael's predicament and hoped that he could help. Janet knew that Rachael wouldn't ask for help herself. She was far too independent to do that. She also guessed that Rachael didn't know the extent of Joshua's influence in business and agricultural circles. If anyone could help, it was her big brother. Unfortunately, Joshua didn't pick up his phone. She tried a few more times with no success, so she decided to seek out James in the meantime and start learning more about the family business, hoping that Joshua would call back as soon as he could.

* * * *

The early morning Wednesday meeting had dragged. It was noon before Joshua could check his BlackBerry for any messages. He saw that there were several missed calls from Janet and immediately called back. He listened quietly while she told him about the Crossling situation and Rachael's problem with the Veterinary Association.

"I'm sorry to disturb you at work, but I thought you'd want to know. I've seen the way you are together, and I know that she's becoming important to you."

"She is. Thanks for letting me know. I'll call Colin and see what can be done. Don't mention this to Rachael."

He'd be damned before he let Crossling hurt Rachael's professional reputation. He knew how important it was to her. He also knew that he was acting out of self-interest. If Rachael couldn't practice in Texas, she may think about leaving, and he didn't know if their fledgling relationship was strong enough yet to keep her here without her work. It was time to call in a few favors and secure Rachael's position.

* * * *

Mitch had managed to get a few hours sleep, but he was unsettled and couldn't get his mind off Janet. Her revelation last night had shocked him because he had assumed that she had lost her virginity long ago. Her brothers were not exactly slackers in that department, and he again had assumed that she had few inhibitions regarding sex. Well, it appeared she had one—him. Janet had waited for him and that made him feel ten feet tall and worried at the same time. He was not a small man, and he knew from experience that his cock was much thicker than average. How was he going to make love to Janet, a virgin, and not hurt her? He decided to do some Google research.

Mitch found a lot of information on the subject. It appeared that, for some women, the first time could be painful, and there would be blood when the hymen torn, but for others there was no pain at all, particularly those who had been active cycling or horse riding because the hymen was already broken. The more that he read, the more he realized that all women were different but that lots of foreplay and lubrication were always recommended. Well, at least he could do that. He loved to do that, but it still didn't solve the issue of his size. Even if she weren't a virgin, his girth would still be a problem but less so because her muscles would have already been stretched. With male logic, he reasoned that they needed to begin with something smaller than his dick. Obviously, a vibrator or dildo of some kind would be ideal but there was a snag. He didn't have one and, as deputy of police, he sure as hell wasn't waltzing into the local sex shop to acquire one. He racked his brain for a solution. What could he use that would progressively stretch her with the minimum of discomfort? He grabbed his keys and headed out to the grocery store.

* * * *

By late afternoon, Janet had finished making notes about some of the new things she had learned that day. She decided that there was definitely material here that she could use in her last assignment, scheduled for the end of April before the final examinations. She could kill two birds with one stone: learn more about the family business and get good research done for her studies.

She closed her laptop, sighing because she had found it hard to concentrate, her thoughts constantly returning to Mitch and what they were planning to do that night. She was excited and a little nervous, not because she wasn't ready—she was most definitely ready—but because she realized that Mitch was a big man. The only way it wasn't going to hurt was if he couldn't get it in. *If I'd known, I might have gone out and got myself laid in preparation.* But even as she thought it, she knew it wasn't true. Lots of boys had expressed an interest, but she had never wanted to make love to any of them; all she thought about was the deputy, with his gun belt strapped on and his tight, sexy trousers. Just as she was daydreaming about him again, her cell rang, and it was Mitch.

"Hi, Jan, you okay? Still on for tonight?" He sounded almost anxious.

"Absolutely. Did you get some sleep?"

"Some, but I've been a bit preoccupied."

"Oh, really? Funnily enough, so have I."

He chuckled. ''Do you want me to come and pick you up?"

"No, I'll head out at six o'clock. I can't wait to see you."

"Likewise, but no speeding, I don't want Officer McGowan to detain you."

"Okay, see you later.'

"Janet, wait. Listen. Remember what you said about being imaginative?"

"How can I forget?" She groaned.

"Well, just bear that in mind. I'll see you soon."

What was that about?

She decided to first take a shower and do all the messy jobs like shaving and exfoliating and washing her hair. She was uncertain what Mitch's preference was regarding pubic hair, so she decided to simply trim the area, reasoning that it would be quick and easy to take more off, but would take longer to grow it back. Then she took a long, hot bath filled with delicious strawberry-scented oil. Thinking of Mitch, she couldn't resist touching herself as she soaked in the warm water. Getting more and more turned on, she decided that it might be a good idea to try to stretch her internal channel a bit.

She got out of the bath and rummaged around in her private drawer that she kept locked. Great, there was the bright pink, slender vibrator that Macy, her best friend at college, had given to her as a joke one Christmas. Macy had expected her to unwrap it in front of her brothers. Luckily, Janet has guessed what it was before opening it. Her friend hadn't been so fortunate with the butt beads Janet had given her. Macy had to pretend to her parents that they were a bracelet. Janet had to admit that Macy's gift had turned out to be useful. The batteries were now flat, but she didn't need it to vibrate for her purposes. After two minutes, she changed her mind and hunted for some AAAs.

Temporarily satisfied, Janet stood staring at the contents of her underwear drawer. It was sadly lacking in the sexy lingerie department. All her matching sets were a bit too pink and girlie, which was definitely not the look she was going for. Mitch had seemed to appreciate her panties last night, so she chose another white lace thong and a matching bra. She opted for black jeans and a white camisole top that laced up the front. Did Mitch prefer her hair up or down? It never bothered her before. He seemed to like it however she wore it. Jesus, she needed to get a grip and calm down and stop dithering. She decided to leave it loose because it made her look older and very different from the little girl image he might still have of her.

Before leaving the house, Janet tracked down James.

"I'm seeing Mitch tonight, and I won't be home. I'm just letting you know so that you don't come screeching through Ridge Water conducting a search and rescue for me." She gave him a reassuring hug.

"Just, you know, be careful. Make sure he uses—" He sounded like he was choking.

"A condom? "

"Yeah."

"Of course, now this is getting weird, so I'm off. See you tomorrow."

It *was* weird to be reminded about safe sex by James, but who else would? Their parents were dead, and Joshua wasn't here. When she thought about it, she began to realize just how much of a parent Joshua had been to her. When she had first asked about where babies really came from, Joshua had sat down and given her "the talk." When she had her first period, Joshua bought the sanitary products and made her feel special. James had helped, of course, but he was four years younger than Joshua and it had made for a big difference in the level of maturity. Well, they were all grown up now, and she thought that under the circumstances her brother hadn't done a bad job. She bounced happily out of the house

Janet arrived at Mitch's home twenty-five minutes later, having stayed at the speed limit almost the entire journey. She parked her SUV in his driveway and got out, grabbing her overnight bag. Mitch must have heard the engine because he appeared in his doorway and strolled out to meet her.

He looked spectacular in a torso-hugging white T-shirt, a tight pair of black jeans, and heavy, black biker-type shoes. Clean yet rough and tough. Janet's heart began to race. She was used to being around big, good-looking men, so she knew buff when she saw it. Mitch was a broad solid man with bulging muscles. At five feet ten inches, she often felt tall and clumsy with the boys at college. Not with this man. He dwarfed her. She felt fragile compared to his hulking frame. He obviously took time to train and keep fit. She bet he had good stamina, something she hoped to have intimately confirmed.

* * * *

"Baby, you look gorgeous. Come here." He loved her long flowing hair and just wanted to run his fingers through it and twist it around his hands and——

"We match," she said indicating to their clothes and dragging him from his fantasy. He pulled her to him and gave her a gentle welcome kiss on the mouth, restraining all the pent-up need and desire he had for her. She gently teased her tongue along his lips, deepening the kiss and invading his mouth. Some of his tightly bound desire unravelled, and they were soon devouring each other on the doorstep.

"Let's take this inside," he growled deeply.

Mitch easily picked her up and carried her into a spacious open-plan room consisting of a lounge, dining and kitchen area. She started to kiss him again, and he held her tightly to his broad chest. Although small compared to him, she was solid and strong just the way he liked. He cautioned himself to be extra gentle with her because tonight would be her first time. He sat her gently on the sofa and crouched down at eye level in front of her. He held both of her hands in his, caressing them with his thumbs.

"Last night you said that you loved me." Janet looked at him with sparkling sapphire blue eyes, searching for the truth.

"I did. I do."

"I have loved you from a distance for as long as I can remember, and I think that I always will." Her voice was as soft as a summer night's breeze.

The situation was so different to the normal casual relationships and sex that he had indulged in before. So much more was at stake here—her heart and his. Her happiness and well being were paramount to him.

"I need to ask you a few questions. It'll help me to…do this right, okay?"

She nodded.

"Have you ever had anything wider than my finger inside you?"

He saw a rose flush creep across her face. She looked at his thick, chunky fingers and shook her head.

"No, not wider but a bit longer."

"Okay. It's likely that your hymen has already been breached and will have disintegrated, especially because you ride a lot." He regretted sounding like a family doctor. "If it is still intact, do you mind it being broken by me but not with my cock?"

"I just want you. I don't care about some layer of skin. I only haven't had intercourse because I couldn't get you out of my head, not because of some old-fashioned notion of purity."

Wow. She really had waited for him. "Good. Janet, I want to take care of you. You're precious to me. When we make love, it's gonna be so good between us, but we have to take this nice and slow. I'm not a small man. I don't want to hurt you."

"I've felt you, and I know that you're not bragging. I think I'm going to be a lucky woman. No gain without pain, right?" She smiled nervously.

"Baby, there's sometimes a thin line between pain and pleasure, but tonight I want to take it easy and we'll enjoy ourselves, okay? No pressure."

"Your right, I suppose there's no rush." She didn't sound convinced.

"Exactly." But, by God, he didn't want to wait. He wanted to be joined in the flesh with her, to hear her screams of ecstasy.

"Now, baby, I'm gonna show you something. You might be surprised, but I think it's a way forward. Keep an open mind. I've been shopping." He led her to the kitchen counter, wary of her reaction.

"You're kidding!" she shrieked.

There, lined up, was a banana and thick cucumber, and each had a condom next to it. She started to giggle.

"When James mentioned using a condom, I don't think he had this in mind." She started to laugh in earnest. "Jesus, Mitch, your imagination has been working overtime, I'm just," she was trying to catch her breath, "I'm just glad you didn't raid the squash section." She howled with laugher.

"I'm glad you're taking this seriously." He was trying to frown but was failing. He loved the sunshine in her, the uninhibited joy. It and her laughter were infectious and soon the two of them were rolling around on the floor.

"I'm sorry, I just can't stop thinking how you must have furtively foraged in the fruit section and perversely prowled the produce. Oh, God, my stomach hurts. I'll never be able to go to Mel's Mart again without blushing. If only they knew what sinister fate awaited their groceries." Another fit of giggles consumed her. "I'm not at all sure I want to lose my virginity to Carl the Cucumber, no matter how handsome he is!"

"Laugh it up, babe, laugh it up. You'll be thanking me later."

When she calmed down, she asked, "Mitch, why can't you just use your fingers?"

How fucking obvious. He could kick himself.

"I guess I was thinking about a smaller version of my cock, a vibrator or a dildo. I thought that the shape might make it…smoother, easier. I missed the obvious." If he used his fingers he would be able to feel her muscles relax, he would know her response better.

She gave him a heartwarming smile.

"You've been so preoccupied about my comfort that you've forgotten the simple fact that I'm a woman and you're a man and our bodies are designed to fit. I knew there must be a reason I've got hips like these." She waggled her curvy ass. "You worry too much, Deputy."

"Only about you." He looked at her sprawled out next to him, red-faced and breathless from laughing and imagined she'd look similar after sex—irresistible.

"I know, and thank you, but I want you, not a salad. Now, you have me on the floor, horizontal. Whatcha gonna do about it?" she goaded.

It was a good time to show her properly what all the fuss was about. He undid his belt and unzipped his jeans as he lay on the floor next to her. She watched in interest as he hooked his thumbs in the waistband of both his boxers and pants and pushed them down.

"Wow, oh my—wow." She gulped, unable to look away from his canon-like cock. "Obviously, I wasn't paying enough attention last night," she whispered, finally having the good sense to look nervous.

"Don't worry," he assured her gently. "I'll take good care of you, but you see why I went to the trouble?"

She didn't say anything for a few seconds, and then blurted out, "There's an elephant somewhere missing a trunk. Get Carl."

He laughed. "We'll try fingers first, shall we? We've plenty of time."

They began, there and then, on the soft rug on the floor, their laughter turning to groans as they thoroughly explored each other, stripping away the layers of clothing between them.

Mitch marvelled at her soft skin and curves; she had those aplenty and he appreciated it. She had a nice, rounded ass, hips he could firmly hold, and large tits that filled even his huge paws. He wanted to hold her to him and feel her softness against his hardness. The heat of their bodies merged and he was distinctly aware of her scent mixing with his own. It was a heady combination and he breathed in deeply through his nose, wanting to experience all of the woman who lay under him. He kissed his way down her neck to her generous breasts and sucked gently on each nipple, teasing each to hard, sensitive nubs.

"You're perfect." He smiled as he cupped and gently squeezed a breast in one big hand. He continued his way south, kissing her flat stomach and curvy hips, caressing her smooth, soft skin, touching her with butterfly-light caresses. He stroked her thighs, bent her legs, and opened them wide. The delicate, sensitive folds of her pussy hid her opening like the closed petals of a flower at night. He bent forward and parted them with his tongue; Janet moaned and tilted her hips. He licked along the seam up to her clit and lightly tickled the succulent hood with his tongue.

"Oh, oh, that feels amazing," she groaned.

He made a noise of appreciation deep in this throat as he tasted her. He hadn't been mistaken last night; it was the most delectable treat he'd ever known. The thought that she was his, that her pussy would be on the menu for him anytime, caused his blood to heat and his cock to get even harder; not necessarily a good thing under the circumstances. She threaded her fingers through his hair and gently pulled him away. Her eyes held an ocean of yearning in their depths.

"I–I'm not very experienced, but I want to give you the same pleasure that you give me," she said shyly.

Didn't she know that just being there with him, allowing him to love her, was pleasure enough? This night was all about her.

"You don't have to do anything baby. Just relax and let me make love to you."

"But I want—I *need* to touch you, too. Mitch, sixty-nine. I want to taste and suck you."

Lord Almighty. How could he refuse?

"Sit on my face," he said in a raspy voice, and turned to lie on his back.

She grabbed the tube of lube off the table as she moved to reposition herself.

"Oooh, strawberry flavor, how thoughtful," she delightedly exclaimed as she crouched over him.

Quickly, she spread the gel-like substance onto her right palm. She leaned over, resting her weight on one elbow, and took as much of a hold of his chunky cock as she could. Her grip didn't nearly reach around him, so she twisted her hand with each stroke, clenching and sliding around him as she pumped her hand slowly up and down his length.

"God, that's so good, baby. That's just right," he growled before pulling her hips down and her pussy closer.

Although she was moist, he grabbed the lube that she had left on the floor and coated his fingers. While he continued to lick and tease her clit, he pushed his middle finger slowly inside. Her tight muscles gave way, and he slid back and forth in a slow motion, pressing against the sides of her hot muscular walls. He decided to try two fingers so he withdrew his hand, crossed his middle finger over the index, and entered them into her again. It was a little harder, but he slid inside and slowly spread his fingers apart. He felt her muscles tense but then relax as he tongued her clit in a circular motion.

Still gripping his cock, she kissed the large head and swirled the flat of her tongue around it before tickling with the tip under the rim. He made a deep noise of approval, enjoying her hesitant yet thorough investigation.

Starting with a kiss on the top, she slowly took him into her mouth and slid slowly down his length. He could feel her lips widening and tightening around him as he filled her mouth to capacity.

"Breathe through your nose, baby. Don't take me too deep." He didn't want her to gag or feel uncomfortable. There would be plenty of time later for lessons in how to deep throat a large cock. Tonight her hand would have to do most of the work, and he wasn't complaining because it was sublime. With tender finesse, she maintained a firm, steady pumping action on his shaft. Her oral effort was focused on the large, sensitive, plum-sized head.

Mitch knew that he was going to come soon, so he began to tongue her clit more vigorously and move his fingers deeper and a little faster. He could tell that she was near to climax as she lost some of her tossing rhythm and made small, panting, gasping cries. He was so close to coming his balls were tightening, but he only had to hold off a few more seconds. She jerked and trembled, and her pussy clamped around his fingers. She held his cock tight and gave a muffled shriek with her mouth still around the head. He cried out and bucked his hips, filling her mouth, as her juices coated his face, buried between her trembling thighs.

After a minute, she scooted around and collapsed on top of him. They stayed that way awhile, floating in a postorgasmic stupor. He kissed her, registering the fact that he had come in her mouth.

"Sorry, sweetheart. I should have said spit or swallow."

"I did a bit of both. Your face is wet. Is that me?"

He licked his lips. "Yep, delicious."

She sat up, straddling him. "Did I—was it okay. I'm not that experienced."

"No, it wasn't okay. It was perfect." She was perfect. He stroked her face then moved his hands down her sides and between her legs. "You're very slick and relaxed. Let's see if we can make it three." He wiggled his fingers in front of her.

"Okay." She nodded and splayed her thighs a bit wider.

She displayed nothing but trust, and he was going to make darn sure it wasn't misplaced. Watching her face the whole time, he put his thumb, index, and middle finger close together and gently pressed them into her flesh. Although tight, it was much more pliant than before, and he was steadily able to press deeper. At one point, she winced and he felt her muscles contract. He smiled encouragingly at her.

"Relax, baby, relax," he coaxed. "Yeah, that's right, let it go."

Her muscles eased off, and he was able to slowly move deeper until he was up to the third knuckles. He pumped his hand gently to get her channel accustomed to the invasion and then slowly splayed his fingers, pushing against the strong muscles of her cunt.

"Oh," she moaned.

"Does it hurt?" He stopped.

"Not really. It's good."

He moved his fingers in and out a little faster and gave her clit attention with his other hand. Within a minute, she was panting and meeting his thrusting hand with her hips.

"Agh, I'm coming again," she cried, rearing up on his chest and gripping his shoulders as she pushed herself farther onto his hand and came. She jerked as her cunt spasmed around his splayed open fingers.

"Oh, God, I have to have you. Mitch. I'll die of want if I don't."

"Baby, you look so beautiful. I can't wait until my cock's inside you. It will be tonight, I promise." He was hard again already.

"Not later, now, Mitch, now," she pleaded

"Are you sure?" He wasn't convinced that she was could take him but he wasn't about to argue because his weapon was cocked tight and ready to go again.

"Yes, I want it," she demanded.

"Stay on top, at least until I'm in. You can control the entry. Use lots of lube." This way, he wouldn't get too carried away and she could dictate the pace. "Oh, and don't forget a condom."

* * * *

She reached up and snatched a foil-wrapped condom next to the cucumber. "Sorry, Carl, buddy, you're out of luck."

Janet tore open the wrapper and noticed the extra-large sizing. *You got that right.* Using two hands, she smoothly rolled it over his very taut dick. Now for the lubrication, lashings of it—her pussy would be strawberry flavored for hours.

"I'll help support you," Mitch said, and placed his big hands on her hips as she squatted over him.

Janet reached down and positioned his cock in line with her hungry cunt. So long she had waited, but no more. She slowly began to descend on him. The large, round, purple head was nestled between her plump pussy lips, which parted like a mouth stretched in an expression of wide exclamation as she slowly fed herself his cock. She felt the first pull of her soft tissues over his hard, solid, slippery shaft. It wasn't painful— not yet. She breathed deeply then continued slowly, slowly until the first pinch of pain struck. She stopped, unsure what to do.

"Help me, Mitch."

"Back up a bit, babe, just a bit," he gently advised.

She did as he bid her and the sharp pinching sensation eased.

"Let's relax those muscles a bit more, shall we? Use your knees to support yourself. Yeah, that's right. It's a good thing you've got long legs."

Once she was settled and could relax her leg muscles more, he began to play with her clit. Like a master conductor, he controlled her body, bringing her toward the ultimate crescendo. She gave herself over to him because she knew he would take care of her. She tilted her head back, feeling wild and wanton.

"So fucking beautiful," he growled at the lush sight of her. "Take more of my cock, Janet."

Again, she began to descend onto him, but this time she felt a need greater than her fear of pain and sank farther. He continued to lightly rub her clit with a well-lubricated finger and spoke to her in a voice dripping with desire. "I want you riding my fat cock to oblivion, babe. Soon, you'll be so stuffed full of my cock that you'll never want any other man ever. You saved the best for first, Janet."

Yes. After this, she would never underestimate the power of the mind as an aphrodisiac.

"Oh, God," she half yelped, half gasped as she slid farther down his length. Her orgasm loomed and demanded completion. She needed him all the way inside, not just the two inches of ground gained.

"Mitch, just thrust into me. Do it quickly, do it now," she cried.

"No way, Janet. I'll not hurt you that way." His jaw muscle twitched as he gritted his teeth.

It drove her insane. She needed all of him. When the contractions in her cunt began, they swept away any doubt. When the full force of her orgasm hit, she jerked and fell, plunging herself onto him, screaming in both pleasure and pain.

"Janet!" he cried, holding her still, not moving.

At first it felt as if she were impaled much too deeply upon him and her pussy and womb protested with an intense cramping pain. She didn't dare move, but the pain receded relatively quickly. She began to relax and feel more comfortable.

"I'm okay," she half panted, half sobbed, "just give me a moment."

* * * *

It almost resolved the problem of his size and libido in an instant. He felt wretched and ashamed because he was close to emptying his balls into her as she'd cried out in agony. Even so, her pussy was warm and clenched tightly, vigorously quivering around his embedded cock. It urged him on, tempting him to move. He agonized over what to do. His cock was on a hair trigger, but he didn't want to shoot—not this way, not with her, not the first time.

"Janet, baby, are you okay? Why did you do that?"

He was distraught with concern for her.

"The pain is passing. The pleasure's still there. I've waited long enough; I want all that you can give. Make love to me, Mitch."

Oh, God. He couldn't resist. The unrelenting pressure of her cunt clamped around his restless dick like a sprung trap was taking its toll. His butt clenched as he sought to stave off the inevitable for as long as necessary. He pulled her head down to his, her curtain of soft, dark hair falling about his shoulders. He kissed her, thoroughly exploring her mouth, nibbling her bottom lip and kissing her face. He rolled her underneath him and then sat up with her on his lap. She hissed with the slight shift in position, but smiled and mouthed that she was okay. In this position, he could stand up and stay within her pussy. She wrapped her legs around him, and he grabbed her ass for extra support as he walked to his bedroom.

He knelt on the edge of his bed and gently lowered her down, staying connected, enclosed within her sheath of tight, soft muscle. Like a gun sliding from a perfectly fitted holster, he partly withdrew. Her muscles contracted behind him, snuggly closing the tunnel to her womb. Covering her, he slowly forged forward, parting the still-reluctant walls, easing himself along her slick channel. It was sensationally exquisite to be gripped so tightly by soft, silky, warm flesh. She gasped, and he felt her pussy clench and relax repeatedly, the temporary paralysis obviously over.

"Not a little girl anymore," he whispered.

He began to stroke slowly in and out, holding back, controlling the pace to one she could contend with. He could have come a dozen times since being fully embedded within her, but he wanted her to fly with him, to hear her scream with orgasmic pleasure, and to make it a first time that she would want to remember.

It didn't take long. She gripped his forearms tightly and raised her knees, squeezing him with her legs, keeping him close. Soft moans and mewls escaped from deep within her throat. Her hips swayed to meet his slow, deep thrusts and the tension in his cock grew like a pulled coil spring. Suddenly, she convulsed as her overstretched pelvic floor muscles contracted over and over again, and her pussy juice gushed, coating his cock. The coil snapped back and pure energy raced throughout him, sparking synapses and nerve endings never before so excited.

He covered her mouth with his and stole her climatic scream. He had to have his release now. It was more than enough to hear her moans, to feel her beneath him, to see her passion slackened face, but as she climaxed, her pussy tightened farther around him. He came hard with her name on his lips and his heart in her hands.

He pulled her into a close embrace, murmuring words of love and praise. When he finally floated down to earth his bliss was stolen by the feel of fat tears dripping onto his chest and the sound of a tiny sniffle.

"Oh God, Janet, are you okay? Are you really hurt? I'm sorry, so sorry," he said, panicking and feeling wretched.

"Shut up, you're ruining our moment. I'm just so happy I could burst. It was everything I thought it would be and more. It surely can't get much better than that."

He exhaled loudly in relief and satisfaction that he'd made her feel that way.

"I am honored that I was your first. It was wonderful for me, too. Janet, you felt so tight and responsive that I thought that I was going to lose it at one point. I have to warn you, though, baby, that was just an appetizer—a sort of welcome to Mitch. Between us, it'll only get better and better."

"Really?" She looked and sounded awestruck.

"I promise." He kissed her again and withdrew from her body as he rolled her to the side. "I'll just be a minute," he said as he headed for the bathroom to dispose of the condom.

While there, he found a clean washcloth and wet it with warm water; it might help to soothe any aches. She shivered as he gently applied the cloth between her legs, dabbing carefully around her red and swollen entrance.

"Mmm, that feels good."

"I don't want you to be sore. It may be a little tender. For the first few times, we'll need to go gently and slowly. When you can take my cock easily, we'll get more imaginative." He gave her a wicked grin.

Janet chuckled. "I can't wait."

"You'll have to, greedy girl. Now come on, let's grab a beer and have something to eat."

* * * *

They spent the rest of the evening enjoying each other's company and made love for most of the night, but only had full penetrative sex one more time. Mitch seemed delighted that his cock slipped comfortably between her ample breasts and that she quickly mastered the art of sucking a large cock and could maintain a strong, steady grip.

She couldn't get enough of his wicked fingers and talented tongue that drove her to multiple orgasms. When they had full sex again, the little soreness she experienced was overshadowed completely by the divine rapture she felt at being stuffed so full and milking him dry.

She had always thought that Mitch would be a great fuck. He was fit and athletic—he had a great body, and he knew how to use it—but he was also attentive, responsive, and caring, which made him an exceptional lover—her lover. Janet wanted to shout out in joy.

"One thing is certain, you've ruined sex for me with any other man," she gently teased and yawned as they lay wrapped around each other, in his bed.

"There won't be any other man," he murmured, as they drifted off to sleep.

Thursday morning wouldn't slow down in arriving no matter how much Janet wished it. Mitch had to go to work and would be staying on late to give a talk to his colleagues about the course he had attended in Austin. Usually, the guys went out for a few beers after such events, and although Mitch said that he was happy not to join them later, Janet insisted that he should. She had two brothers, and if that had taught her anything at all, it was to give men some room in their lives. They arranged to see each other on Friday evening at Mitch's home again.

She was happy knowing she would see him again soon enough, and, to be honest, it would give her pussy some much-needed recuperation time. She did feel a little sore but was careful not to let on to Mitch, especially when getting into her car. *Ouch.* Nevertheless, she headed home with a beamer of a smile on her face thinking about last night. James was standing on the veranda when Janet drove up to the house. His gaze narrowed as he watched her gingerly get out of the car and walk carefully up the steps.

"Hey, Jan, are you okay?"

"What? I'm fine, why?" She smiled.

"You're—never mind."

"I'm fine, just a little—I'm fine," She felt herself blush and ran awkwardly inside barely catching her brothers curse.

"God damn, I'll kill him."

She whirled around, "Just you listen to me, James Ryden. I love that man and—and—it was, he was—is—fantastic! I'm so happy I could cry, so back off, cowboy, and be glad that I've found a wonderful man like Mitch Mathews."

He stared at her, stunned, his mouth gaping open like a stranded fish. Slowly, a sheepish grin crossed his face.

"You're a Ryden, all right. Sorry, Jan, I'll mind my own business, Josh was right. You're all grown up."

He lifted his hat in a sort of salute and headed across the yard.

I don't believe it. Suddenly the men in her life had woken up and smelled the roses.

Chapter 9

Rachael was a little miffed that Joshua hadn't called but had only sent a brief SMS saying that he wouldn't be home until Friday afternoon. *Out of sight, out of mind.* Then she felt miserable for being mean-minded. Thursday came and went slowly. It was too quiet a day. She went for an early morning run and then worked a bit in her garden before mooching around and reading a book. Hell, what she really wanted to do was go over to Crossling and thrash it out, but that would only make matters worse.

She tried speaking to someone at the Veterinary Association in Houston, but all the committee members were in a meeting. She just hated waiting and not being proactive and decided to at least write a draft letter to the Association explaining her actions. It would be one less thing to do when they had an inquiry into the allegation.

On Friday, just after lunch, Rachael received a call.

"Ms. Harrison? This is Dr. Volkener, president of the American Medical Veterinary Association here in Texas."

"Hello, Dr. Volkener. I'm glad that you called. I rang yesterday to speak to someone about an apparent malpractice allegation." She kept her voice pleasant and calm.

"Yes, I'm calling about that. I wanted you to know that the complaint had been dealt with and the matter dropped. We understand that there is no evidence or even an official complaint in writing. Mr. Farley thoroughly explained the facts, and Mr. Ryden has collaborated what happened."

"Mr. Ryden?" Rachael was astonished. "You've spoken with Mr. Ryden?"

"Yes, he was here yesterday and this morning with Mr. Farley. You are fortunate to have such persistent and influential friends, Ms. Harrison."

"Now wait a minute, Dr. Volkener. I'm grateful, very grateful for the case being dropped, but I didn't do anything wrong. In fact, I saved that horse. I only attended to it alone because it was an emergency. Mr. Crossling has issues beyond my professional involvement with him."

Volkener suddenly sounded flustered. "Yes, of course, Ms. Harrison. I didn't mean to imply that our decision is in anyway inappropriate, but it *has* been faster than it would otherwise have been. Mr. Ryden facilitated the process, I have to be honest."

"Just how did he do that?"

"I'm not at liberty to say."

He sounded uncomfortable, and Rachael realized that it was probably not a good idea to upset the president of the Association to which she wished to belong. "Well, thank you for taking the time to inform me personally. I appreciate it."

"Yes, no problem. Have a nice day. Oh, I nearly forgot. Your license has been granted. You'll receive it in the mail this week. Good-bye."

What the heck? She flopped down on the sofa and looked at the phone handset as if it held the answers. Colin and Joshua were at the Veterinary Association in Houston yesterday and this morning in support of her, and that was probably why she couldn't get through to any of the committee members. She felt utter relief but also a smidgeon concerned at what Joshua had said and done to get such a quick decision. Hell, she knew that she was in the right, and being a pragmatic individual, she wasn't going to let pride get in the way. If Joshua had managed to foil Crossling's plans, then she was thankful for it. She called Colin straight away.

"Where are you?"

"On a plane about to turn my cell phone off."

"Would a certain Mr. Ryden be with you?"

"He's in the cockpit."

Cockpit. Now there's an aptly named place. "Well I just got a call from a Dr. Volkener, who I believe you've recently met."

"Ah, yes, well, you're not supposed to know about that."

"Spill it, Colin."

"Okay, okay. Janet rang Josh, and directly after she told him about the allegation, he flew me out to Houston and insisted on meeting the full committee. I gotta tell you cousin, that man is a force to be reckoned with. He has a lot of influence in business circles here, not just because of the sheer size of the ranch but also the Sweet Oil company. But what really swayed it was the fact that they have some of the best breed stock in America, and Joshua suggested that he would be open to discuss the facilitation of a future cattle genetics research program that the vet association would like to conduct."

"You're kidding!" Rachael was astounded that Joshua would go to such lengths for her.

"I shit you not. He must think a hell of a lot of you, Rachael, that's all I can say."

"Can you put him on?"

"They're just prepping the plane. I'll give him a message, providing it's not too rude." He chuckled.

"Tell him I'm very grateful for his help. Tell him to come to the cabin so that I can thank him personally, okay."

"God, I'll try not to stammer and blush."

"Oh, and send me a sneaky SMS when you land. And thank you, too."

It was late afternoon when Rachael's phone bleeped with an SMS from Colin. She took a shower, shaved, and scrubbed, then dressed carefully in a long, flowing skirt and thin fitted silk blouse. She went outside and took up position on the swing seat on the veranda. Attempting to read a book, but actually reading the same few lines over and over, she found her thoughts wandering to Joshua Ryden and her demonstrating her gratitude.

Half an hour later, she was alerted to the approach of a vehicle by the rumble of an engine. As Joshua parked his UV near her cabin and got out, Rachael stood up and waited on the top step. Just the thought of him charged her desire. Just the sight of him stole her breath—such was the strength of her need for him.

* * * *

He stopped about ten yards away and raked his gaze over her form. He was hit by a wave of blatant possessive lust. He noticed that she wasn't wearing a bra, and her erect nipples poked against the thin material of her blouse, leaving little to his rampant imagination.

He knew that he would do anything to keep her near, and nothing would be too much trouble. He felt the air between them, ozone charged like a tangible, captivating force, intent only on holding her to him. She was unique. She was for him. He was resolved to savour the moment, to tease out the threads of palpable anticipation.

"Remove your panties," he ordered quietly yet firmly, staring at her face without the hint of a smile.

She held his gaze. "No."

She was denying him. It was untenable, and he narrowed his eyes.

"I can't," she purred with a hint of a sexy smile. "I'm not wearing any."

Snap, his resolve broke. He stalked forward and swept her off her feet. Kicking the front door open, he stormed in and placed Rachael on the nearest surface—the table. He stood between her legs and kissed her hard, crushing her lips, claiming her mouth. His big hands roamed everywhere. *Rip*, there went her blouse; *tear*, her skirt was gone. He caught her scent—woman, vanilla, and desire. It drove him to distraction.

He broke contact to pull his shirt over his head and shrug out of his pants and jockeys.

"Take me. Fuck me. Do anything you like," she moaned into his mouth. "Joshua, please, I need you."

Her words enflamed his own need for her to yield to his dominance. It wasn't politically correct, but he knew they both wanted it.

"I'll fuck you, all right. I'll take your mouth, your cunt, and your ass, because they're mine and you owe me. Get on your knees, and show me some gratitude. Suck my cock."

He eyes fluttered closed for a second, and she moaned in response to his raw words. She slid off the table and knelt before him, her face level with his proud, hard shaft and large, hanging balls. Taking his girth firmly in one hand, she tightened it around the base as she licked the glistening red helmet.

"Suck it, Rachael."

She complied, wrapping her lips tightly around his thick dick and sliding it inside her warm, wet mouth to the back of her relaxed throat. Her nostrils flared as she inhaled through her nose. He groaned. She alternated pumping his cock with her hand and her mouth, swirling her tongue under the rim of the bulbous head, grazing her teeth on the sensitive underside.

"Jesus, stop. Enough. You sure know how to do grateful."

He pulled her off him by the hair, put his hands under her arms, and lifted her back onto the table, where he pushed her onto her back and pulled her bottom to the edge. He fell to his knees and forced her legs wide with his shoulders. The scent of her sex drove him crazy. He dived between her thighs and plunged his tongue into her wet, petal-soft folds. She nearly jerked off the table.

He played with the tip of his tongue on her clit, which sent her over the edge.

"Oh, please. Oh please," she sobbed, "I'm begging you. Enter me."

He stood between her wide spread thighs and placed the tip of his cock at her hot, slick entrance. He seductively rubbed back and forth along her slit, lubricating himself in her warm liquid passion.

Rachael closed her eyes and panted, "Begging you. Begging for it."

Her reaction stoked his burning lust higher still. He thrust in, hard and deep, sliding her back from the edge of the table. She grabbed the sides to anchor herself as he repeatedly slammed into her. She screamed another climax, arching her back off the table, thrusting her breasts upwards.

It was divine torture. His balls throbbed, but he wasn't finished yet. Breathing deep and hard, he withdrew from her hot interior and flipped her over onto her stomach, effectively bending her over the table. Shoving her legs wider, he moved between them and rubbed his cock between her buttocks. Lubrication—he needed more. Although she was wet and his cock was glistening with her juices, he wanted to be certain not to cause anything other than a small amount of erotic pain. Spying the olive oil on the kitchen counter, he leaned over and grabbed the bottle, then dripped some of the oil at the top of the crack of her ass. Extra virgin? Not anymore. He slowly pushed his way passed the tight ring of muscle and continued to press home until he was snugly up against her.

"Slow and gentle or hard and fast?"

"Hard and fast."

"'Atta girl."

He gave it to her as they both wanted, pushing his ten and a half inches of male meat repeatedly hard and deep into her dark passage. Again, she howled as another orgasm racked her, only this time he joined her, spurting his release into her.

He leaned forward to kiss her back and neck, his rasping breath settling quickly back to normal.

"Hello, Rachael. I've missed you."

* * * *

Later, they were sitting on her sofa, half dressed and drinking coffee.

"Your support this week—it means a lot to me."

She smiled at him. It was a smile that one gives to a beloved. Although she hadn't said the words out loud, he heard it nonetheless. "I was also acting out of self-interest. I don't want you to leave Meadow Ridge."

"That works for me." She slowly grew serious. "Do you trust me, Josh?"

He thought about it for a few seconds. She was as straight up and as honest a person as any he'd ever met. Why hadn't he told her that he loved her? Was he protecting himself if she didn't feel the same way? Where was the trust in that?

"Yes, I do. I love you, Rachael."

She nodded and smiled. "Good. Now how about a game of poker. Same rules?"

He was stunned for a second. He'd just declared himself, and she'd brushed over it. What was she up to? She certainly kept him guessing, but he didn't think that she was stringing him along. What a fascinating creature she was.

"Okay."

This time, Rachael won. Joshua was shocked. He'd played well, but she'd played better. Or had she? Rachael did her best to look pleasantly surprised. He wasn't fooled. He would have to check those cards out later.

"Will there be many ranch hands around at your place?"

"No, it's a Friday night. They'll all be in town."

"What about Janet and James?"

"Janet's at Mitch's and James is out with Luke. He'll be back late."

"Good. Come on, you're driving me home.

Rachael had changed into a skimpy top, tight leggings, and knee-high boots. She had brought along her workbag. He was intrigued but not concerned—not yet, anyway.

When they pulled up outside of the ranch house, she ordered him to take a shower and to "be thorough." Fair's fair. He did as she commanded but quickly because curiosity had him by the balls. When he'd finished, he strolled into the living room wearing jeans and a fresh T-shirt.

"All yours."

"Hands by your side and don't move."

Rachael circled him, inspecting him like a prized animal. She ran her hands across his chest, over his ass, and along the length of his erection straining against his jeans. He almost reached out for her, but she stepped back and shook her head.

"Follow me."

She turned and grabbed her black vet's bag and walked outside and across to the stables without checking to see that he was following. This behavior was new to him. He usually led, and others followed.

The soft, yellow light was already on in the stable. Once they entered, she locked the door behind them.

"Stand over there." She pointed to the railing where they tied the horses at the back of the stall. He sauntered over, confident that he could turn the tables any time he liked.

She bent down, opened her bag, and took out his own cuffs, the ones he had used on her almost a week ago.

"Face the wall and hold the metal railing."

Interesting but nothing new. He wasn't worried, and he was enjoying himself. Rachael tied the chained cuffs on his wrists to the rail. He wasn't going anywhere now.

"Watch me, Joshua."

She next pulled her white work jacket out of her bag. That got a reaction.

"What are you up to, Rachael?" His eyes narrowed as she put on her coat.

"You don't ask the questions here."

She walked in front of him, between his out stretched arms and kissed him gently, winked at him, and then undid his jeans. She pushed then down around his ankles, which acted as bindings for his legs. She noticed with appreciation that his cock was fully engorged and took a long, languorous lick. After rummaging in her bag again, she brought out a pair of latex gloves.

"Rachael." He sounded concerned now, but his dick was still like granite.

She chuckled softly, keeping herself within his field of vision and taking her time to pull the gloves on. She walked behind him, and then he heard a slurping noise, the sound of lots of gel being squeezed from a tube.

"What are you doing? I'm not sure about this."

"I am. Trust me."

She was still behind him and moved in closer, crushing her body against his butt. She reached around his waist, grasped his cock in a strong grip with a well-lubricated hand and began to firmly slide it up and down. He groaned. She squeezed his sac, none too gently either. He was so turned on that he didn't think that he would last long. Suddenly she backed off a little and her other hand moved in a different direction. It glided passed his balls and to his anus. The sensation was exquisite, but his apprehension also grew. As if sensing this, she reassured him.

"Don't worry. I'm a doctor," she said in a soft, husky voice.

"An animal doctor," he croaked.

"Ah, love, aren't you just a hungry wolf?"

She circled her middle finger around the tight constricted muscle of the entrance between his firm buttocks.

"You have such a beautiful ass."

She slowly pressed her finger against the resistant flesh.

"Rachael, I've never—"

"Oh, maybe not such a wolf. Maybe a big pussy…cat."

She'd called him a pussy! He couldn't believe it.

"Now, wait a minute—"

"No, Ryden." Her voice suddenly changed from crooning to harsh. "You don't get to give the orders here. You take them. If I can cope with your meaty member up my ass, you sure as hell can take my finger. Now bend forward and grip the rail."

She continually pumped his cock slowly and applied more pressure with her finger, pushing through the opening. He gasped at the pleasure and slight pain. She waited for a moment then moved her hand slowly backwards and forwards, pushing a little farther each time until she was all the way inside up to her third knuckle. He couldn't help but move his hips. He was beginning to gasp.

"Jesus, what are you trying to do to me?" His voice was strained with desire.

She didn't miss a beat. "Trying? No, I wouldn't call it an attempt. I'm going to make you lose control like you've never done before. For once in your life, you are going to have someone else take over, and you're going to enjoy it. I'm going to fuck you like you've never been fucked before. You'll come so hard you won't be able to stand."

He was confused. The very notion of placing himself in such a vulnerable position part worried and part excited him.

Rachael rhythmically moved her finger, stimulating the sensitive area around his opening.

"You're always the boss—the one who looks after everyone else and takes all the responsibility. You're dominant and assured, and there's nothing wrong with that. I like it. But you don't have to be that way all the time in all areas of your life. Wouldn't it be nice to just give up a little control now and then? We are switching for tonight. I'm taking care of you."

He was breathing hard as she sought out his prostate gland with her finger. Carefully, she applied gentle pressure, massaging the sweet spot deep inside.

"Christ!" he cried out. "Rachael it feels—incredible, like nothing—" he cut off with a groan.

She reduced the pressure of her finger. "Did you know," she said, softly and seductively, "that I can keep you on the brink of orgasm, on the very brink of ejaculation, yet give you almost unending stimulation this way?"

"Oh, God, I do now."

He felt an almighty powerful pressure in his balls. He was attaining a much higher pre-orgasmic state than ever before, yet still the stimulation continued, which was taking him further. He shook, and it felt as if his balls were vibrating, as if fluid was thundering up his cock in explosive pulses—only it wasn't. It was seeping seminal fluid, weeping steadily, accompanied by an excruciatingly slow, burning pleasure. The feeling didn't stop; it went on and on, rolling over him in waves of blissful ecstasy.

"Please, Rachael. Please let me come," he pleaded—he *never* pleaded.

"In a little while."

She gave two more minutes of unsurpassed stimulation before taking pity on him.

"I love you, Joshua Ryden. Now, I'll let you come," she said as she gently rubbed his male G-spot a little harder. At the same time, she took a firmer grip of his cock and pumped it faster.

His heartbeat pounded in his ears as he roared and jerked his body, rattling the rail that he was secured to. Streams of hot semen jetted away from his body onto the straw on the floor. His knees buckled, and he collapsed onto them, supported by the rail and cuffs around his wrists. She went down with him. He could hardly breathe. He certainly couldn't say anything as she slowly removed her finger, stripped off the glove, and threw it into her bag.

She removed her jacket and gently tousled his hair as she walked around him to release him from the cuffs. Rachael crouched next to him and put her arms around his sweat-sheened body, raining soft, light kisses on his shoulder, his neck and his hair. As he slowly recovered, he hugged her to him. The emotional release cause by such a euphoric climax and the declaration of love from the woman in his arms had him desperately blinking back the tears threatening to engulf him. Never, ever had he felt this way. When he was sure that he had a handle on himself, he pulled back and looked at his woman.

"You'll have to marry me now, Rachael."

"Are you proposing to me? You could just be a little affected by recent events." She gently grinned, tenderly stroking his face.

"I'm definitely affected by recent events, and, yes, I am proposing."

"No, you can't. Do it later. Otherwise, what will we tell our kids when they ask about how Dad asked Mom to marry him?"

"Okay, I'll pick a suitable setting." He grinned like the Cheshire cat because she'd really just said yes.

They went back to the house and spent the rest of the night wrapped in each other's arms. In the dark late hours, she had stroked his body and whispered, "I've waited my whole life for you."

"I'm older, so I've waited longer," he'd whispered sleepily in reply.

"You know, Josh, I've an awful lot of fantasies concerning you and me."

"I've got more."

"That's certainly one of the many reasons why I love you."

* * * *

It was nine thirty in the morning when James strolled into the kitchen and found Rachael and Joshua finishing breakfast. He knew it was childish, but he just couldn't stop the huge smirk that was developing on his face.

"Good morning, all. I've just been seeing to the horses. You really should be more careful what you leave lying around, Josh." He placed the cuffs on the table. "Very careless of you, brother, tut-tut." He turned to Rachael. "I'm scolding Joshua because it appears that you were a little tied up last night."

He couldn't wait to see her reaction. Such moments made life more enjoyable. Odd though, it was Joshua who was blushing, staring at the cuffs looking lost in thought. Rachael looked him directly in the eye.

"Oh, dear, but I can't let Josh take the blame. You see, I wasn't the one tied up." She smiled sweetly at him as she leaned over to retrieve the evidence.

What? His amused smugness took a nose dive as shock at the implication of Rachael's words sank in. He stared at them both with his mouth open. Joshua raised his eyes to meet his, and in an unspoken communication, James knew that his brother was in deep.

Rachael got up from the table.

"I'll just put these away, shall I?"

"You lucky bastard," he muttered to Joshua.

She trailed her hand over Joshua's shoulders as she walked passed him toward his rooms. Josh smiled and said only a characteristically short "Yep," then pushed his chair back and followed her.

"Rachael," James called, "you don't have any single friends, do you?"

* * * *

Later that day, Joshua took Rachael riding to a beautiful spot near the river. When they dismounted, he looked like he was about to give a speech.

"Wait." She backed away from him slowly, feeling mischievous. "I'll only listen to you if you can catch me and *make* me listen."

Not giving him a second longer to react, she spun around and ran, dodging through the trees. He'd have to work for it because she was fit and fast. After two minutes of hard sprinting, she slowed a little and looked over her shoulder. Where was he? She was sure that the chase would be a favorite fantasy of his, but he'd disappeared. She scanned the area and tried to bring her breathing under control so that she could listen better. Suddenly, she heard a twig snap and saw a blur of movement up ahead. How the hell had he managed to get around and ahead of her? She reacted quickly, dodging around a fallen tree. He easily vaulted over it. She adopted a zigzag pattern to avoid capture as she heard his heavy breathing and the thud of his feet on the ground. The gap between them was closing.

Strong fingers gripped her shoulder and yanked her back. For a brief moment, she was airborne as he pulled her roughly to him with an arm locked firmly around her waist and her feet off the ground. Rachael struggled in earnest, twisting her body and flailing her arms and legs. Joshua dropped them both to the ground, sat on her, yanked her arms above her head, and held them in a viselike grip to avoid her punches and slaps. She bucked and squirmed. He covered her body with his. She was pinned.

"You're fucked now, Rachael," he snarled.

She was panting and her face was flushed, but it wasn't the physical exertions that had her nipples pebbling and her cunt creaming. It was the embodiment of her sexual fantasies lying over her.

"You will submit."

She still struggled as he crushed her lips with his mouth and forced his tongue inside. He clasped one hand around both wrists and used the free one to hold her jaw while he took her mouth with a brutal kiss. The wildness inside of her clawed to get out. A switch tripped, and she found herself meeting his tongue with her own, pushing back; grinding her hips against his groin. He lifted his weight a little, and she wrapped her legs around him.

"No, Rachael, that's not submitting. If I was prepared, I'd have you staked by now," he growled.

Staked? Oh, my God. Rachael moaned at the erotic image and Joshua smiled wickedly when he heard her response.

"Another time, darlin'. I promise. Now, do you give in?"

* * * *

He looked down at his adorable, beautiful woman. All that struggling, grunting and cursing had left her flushed and looking aroused. By God, he loved her and her little games. He especially appreciated the chase. It fed his base desires.

She nodded.

"Don't move."

He pulled her jeans down and opened his own, then flipped her over. She couldn't help wiggling her ass and grinding up against him.

Slap. "Ow!"

"I said, don't move. Don't speak, either. Only yes or no."

Her white butt blossomed red where he had smacked her. Her succulent folds glistened, and he didn't need to check her readiness. She was always ready for him, and he was perpetually aroused by her. He positioned his rock-hard cock and plunged into her all the way, balls deep. She gasped.

"Now I'm *making* you listen. We are gonna spend the rest of our lives together, and it's gonna be fucking fantastic. Agreed?" He spoke through gritted teeth as he forged into her repeatedly.

"Yes," she cried.

"We'll get married soon, at Sweet Water, within the next two months. That should allow your friends and family time to make preparations for getting here. I'll pay for the flights. You will not concern yourself about the cost."

"But"—*slap*—"ow! Yes, okay, yes."

"You can work full- or part-time, whatever you want."

"Yes."

"We'll give ourselves a year or two before babies. In that time, I'll fuck you like the bitch in heat that you are." His voice broke with a groan as her slick channel tightened around him.

"Yes," she panted.

"You'll be a professional at the practice, a lady in livingroom, and a complete slut in our bed."

"Yes."

"We'll live at Sweet Water until we build a house either for us or for James and Janet."

"Yes," she shrieked, her legs trembling and her cunt beginning to clench spasmodically.

"I fucking adore you, woman. You'll always be mine." His balls tightened, and he shot his sperm into her, claiming her body as his words claimed her soul.

"Yes!" she howled, shuddering with her own release.

He clutched her to him as they came down slowly from their climax, keeping her firm ass pressed against his muscular thighs.

"Well, I must say, Rachael, you are being very compliant," he drawled, tapping her lightly on the ass. He sounded smug and satisfied.

"You won the right…this time."

He chuckled. There she was with his cock buried deep inside her, still challenging him. She was perfect.

They headed back to the horses and stripped off their clothes to cool down in the fresh, clear river water. Isabella, the housekeeper, had packed a picnic with lots of tasty treats. They sat on a picnic blanket. Joshua was propped up against a boulder with Rachael between his legs leaning against his chest. Half dressed, they ate and chatted, lazily enjoying the late afternoon.

"Okay, now I'm going to do this right."

Joshua shifted, standing up and pulling her with him. He held her hand, got down on one knee, and presented her with an empty box.

"Er, it's traditional in England to actually have a ring," she said, biting her cheek and failing to keep a straight face.

"Well, darlin', I'm having a ring made, but I didn't want to wait."

She leaned over and fondled his balls through his jeans. "These are the only jewels I'm interested in."

"That's certainly one of the many reasons why I love you," he echoed her words of the night before. "Now, Miss Harrison, will you do me the honor of marrying me?"

"Mr. Ryden, yes. I love you so much. How could I not? Now, about those field tests you wanted to conduct…"

Epilogue

Roy Crossling was going to get his hands on *his* oil no matter what. Janet Ryden was under the watchful eye of the deputy and she disliked him now anyway. He'd have to try another way and he had a plan. Meantime, he was pissed that he'd had to sell his best horse cheaply. Secretly in the night, he'd delivered the animal to an address out of the county, and all for nothing because the bitch was now a fully licensed vet, still working with Colin and still living at Flora's Place. The only positive thing was that if she married Ryden, she wouldn't be around the cabin and near his land so much. He didn't want her to discover the illegal drilling he'd started. The sooner she was gone the better. Frustration and hatred smoldered in his belly.

* * * *

Janet was over the moon for her brother and the family. Rachael would not only be a great friend but also a great sister. All this love in the air had her thoughts constantly meandering back to Deputy Mitch Mathews. Things were getting very interesting in bed—well, not only in bed but all over the house, actually, and she knew it wasn't possible to be more satisfied than he made her. She couldn't get enough of the man, but she would soon have to go back to college, and for the first time ever, she didn't relish the thought of leaving. She consoled herself with the fact that it wasn't for long. Her final exams and dissertation would be finished in July, just in time for the wedding. Then she planned on being home, for good, in Meadow Ridge County with Mitch.

* * * *

Shannon O'Reilly was both shocked and delighted to receive a phone call from her best friend Rachael, informing her that she was getting married and wanted Shannon to be the Chief Bridesmaid. She really needed a break from her hectic work schedule and this would be a great opportunity to do just that.

Rachael had sounded excited and very much in love. She wouldn't let it affect their friendship but darn it, why did Rachael have to be marrying a Texan cattle rancher and oil man?

For a few years now, Shannon had laid down her jacket of environmental activism and donned the respectable cloak of an environmental consultant. She thought that she could better instigate changes and promote environmental awareness by lobbying for tighter legislation to protect the environment and educating businesses, rather than chaining herself to railings. It was certainly more comfortable.

She just hoped that this Ryden fellow wasn't an ignorant redneck whom she hated on sight. No, she didn't think that would be Rachael's type. But what did she know? She wouldn't have said that a whirlwind romance was Rachael's modus operandi either. Rachael had mentioned some pretty strange relationship arrangements in the county. It made her quite hot and bothered just thinking about it.

* * * *

James was pleased for his brother. Joshua had been lonely for far too long and had thrown himself into the business to compensate, but now he had a really great woman who seemed to somehow complete him. James couldn't remember seeing his brother so happy. If only he and Luke could find someone like that. A wedding was as good a place as any to do a little pussy hunting. Lots of single ladies at a romantic occasion. Finding Ms. Right would be like hitting the jackpot while playing the slots. *Things may be about to get interesting.*

THE END

dawnforrest@yahoo.com

ABOUT THE AUTHOR

I was born in the industrial North West of England but was lucky enough to spend most of my weekends messing about on my Grandparents' organic farm.

I went to University in Scotland and met my future husband there. We were married, in Florida, in a hot air balloon, and are still married to this day nearly 20 years later; plus two kids.

We have travelled extensively and move internationally with my husband's work. For some time now we have been expats, not staying in one country for more than three years. This had given me the opportunity to meet many wonderful and interesting people, often with fascinating stories to tell.

I try to have fun where ever I am and see humour in most circumstances. I started my first novel in South Africa and finished it in India. I have no idea where we will be in the near future but I intend to keep on writing because I love it. I hope that you enjoy reading my stories and my characters as much as I enjoyed creating them.

Many thanks for reading,
Dawn Forrest

Siren Publishing, Inc.
www.SirenPublishing.com

Breinigsville, PA USA
01 March 2011
256682BV00003B/6/P